/2

SINISTER GRAVES

Books by Marcie R. Rendon

Murder on the Red River
Girl Gone Missing
Sinister Graves

SINISTER GRAVES

MARCIE R. RENDON

Published by
Soho Press, Inc.
227 W 17th Street
New York, NY 10011

Library of Congress Cataloging-in-Publication Data

Rendon, Marcie R., author.
Sinister graves / Marcie R. Rendon.
Series: The Cash Blackbear mysteries ; 3

ISBN 978-1-64129-383-9
eISBN 978-1-64129-384-6

Subjects: LCGFT: Novels.
LCC PS3618.E5748 S57 2022 | DDC 813'.6—dc23/eng/20220128
LC record available at https://lccn.loc.gov/2022003906

Interior design by Janine Agro

Printed in the United States of America

10 9 8 7 6 5 4 3 2 1

#stolenchildren

#mmiw

SINISTER GRAVES

Cash sat in a battered fishing boat on murky floodwater that was headed to the Red River. The spring flood covered the Valley as far to the east and west as she could see. Schools had closed. No one could get to church to pray. The prehistoric, glacial Lake Agassiz existed once again. What had been plowed fields of wheat and corn, soybeans and oats, potatoes and sugar beets were now an ice-cold, snow-melt lake. Sixty miles wide, from one side of the valley to the other.

Cash took a break from oaring, removed a mitten and dipped her hand in the frigid water. If you got caught in the floodwaters, the freezing temperatures would kill you as fast, or faster, than the rushing water. She quickly pulled her hand back out, cupped it near her mouth, and blew warm air over her fingers. Even bundled up in a winter jacket, scarf, mittens and a stocking cap pulled low over her ears, she still shivered in the cold.

Al, a friend of a friend of one of the regular drinkers at the Casbah bar, was sitting in the rear of the boat. Cash carefully turned around on the seat, so she was facing him. He wasn't bad looking. His hair wasn't as long as a hippie's, but not a short farmer buzz either. His skin said Indian. Cash guessed he was a Vietnam vet.

As Al navigated the floodwaters, he would either drop the small motor into the water to move them along faster or bring the motor up when the water was too shallow. At that point, he would oar with her.

Just a week ago, the Red River Valley had been snow-covered. It had been a long winter with whiteout snowstorms that left four-foot road drifts and piles of snow taller than the haystacks in the fields. Then there was one day warm enough for snowmelt. That's all it took—one day in the valley at forty degrees, followed by three more days with temperatures that didn't drop below freezing.

The Wild Rice River, with its headwaters on the far eastern shore of the ancient Lake Agassiz, carried the snowmelt down into the Valley. And when the Wild Rice, along with a hundred other small tributaries, rapidly flooded their banks, all the water moved in a murky rush to spill across the fields of the Valley, the farms and towns, to join the muddy red snake that ran to the north.

Farmers had scrambled to sandbag their barns to keep their cows safe before moving to bag their own homes. Then they rode tractors into town to fill more bags to lay around the perimeters of the small towns; the huge tractor tires kept their bodies safe above the floodwaters.

Cash had spent eleven hours the day before throwing sandbags with a chain of humans—one end filled bags with sand, then ten to fifteen people passed the full bags to those at the end of the line, who laid the sandbags like bricks to create a dike in order to keep the river from flooding downtown Fargo. It was a rush against the forces of nature.

It happened almost every year with the snowmelt. The only questions ever asked were how high would the water rise and how long would it stay. This year was one for the records. Water rose and rose. It overflowed the riverbanks, filled the fields, crept into barns and homes, and the streets of the towns that didn't sandbag fast enough. The floodwaters covered the land from the Red River Valley to Lake Winnipeg, way up north in Manitoba. Farmers prayed for the water to recede in days, not weeks.

When Cash had arrived home after helping fill sandbags, she was so bone-weary she flopped into bed without getting undressed and didn't wake until the incessant ringing of her landline woke her. No one except Wheaton ever called. What few friends she had, had given up on her ever answering her phone. Most just dropped by and hollered up at her apartment. Or made the journey up the flight of stairs and knocked. But that early morning phone call rang and rang. It had stopped briefly, then started ringing again.

Cash finally pushed herself off the bed and stumbled to

the kitchen, where the beige rotary phone sat on the counter. She picked up the handset. "Yeah?"

"Cash, it's Wheaton. What are you doing?"

"Sleeping. There's a flood out there."

Silence.

"What?"

"We have a body here that floated into town."

Silence.

"Where?"

"Ada."

"Highway 75 is flooded. I don't even know if I can get over to Moorhead. Last night, they were saying the river might crest over the bridges in downtown."

"Maybe someone's got a boat that could get you out here."

More silence.

"You'd have to follow the road up. Stay away from the river. River's going too fast to try and get on. Maybe a boat with a motor could get you up Highway 75 or 9—9 might be safer. Water's not as deep, and there really is no current. The water is just sitting on the fields, waiting for the river to empty up north."

Cash had leaned her head against the counter. Her waist-length braid slid over one shoulder. Even though she worked out each week in the judo class at the university, the muscles in her arm holding the phone had been sore from moving sandbags all day. She pulled the headset away from her ear and stared at it.

"Cash?"

"Yeah. Okay." She hung up.

The phone rang again.

"Cash?"

"What?"

"You hung up. Are you coming?"

"I said okay." And she hung up again.

IT HAD TAKEN SOME DOING and a promise of a twelve-pack, but she finally found someone—Al—to ferry her the forty-five miles north. The sky was overcast. The last thing the Valley needed was snow or rain. The clouds didn't look like they were ready to drop any more moisture, but they created a gray mass moving to the east above the muddy floodwater. A depressing, cold day no matter how you looked at it. Occasionally, the small boat had to fight the moving current but, mostly, it was an easy ride traveling north.

Al navigated through the flood-filled ditch along Highway 9. The murky water was about a foot over the pavement, but she could still see the white road lines. Al lifted the motor and he and Cash used the oars to bring the boat to land where the highway met the floodwaters. Al, who was wearing wading boots, jumped out and pulled the boat up and out of the water. He tied it to a highway sign, and they walked the few blocks into town. Al to the local bar, and Cash to the jail.

Wheaton, the county sheriff, was sitting at his desk, his dog, Gunner, lying at his feet. Gunner ignored Cash's entrance. A few months back Wheaton had seen a gunny sack running down a gravel road, which ended up holding a small black mutt inside—probably a mix between a German shepherd and a Lab. Now, Wheaton and the dog were inseparable. Cash was certain the dog resented her presence in Wheaton's life.

Wheaton was eating half a roast beef sandwich. He held the uneaten half up in her direction. They ate in silence—her on the oak bench she considered hers, and him at his desk. Back when she was three, Wheaton had pulled her family out of a ditch that her mother, who had had a few too many beers at the local bar, had rolled her car into. Cash had spent that night, and a few more, sleeping on the wooden bench she now sat on. Shortly after, she'd ended up in the foster care system. Wheaton had been the adult who stayed a constant in her life. Checking in on her, rescuing her again when things had gotten really rough in the last foster home. He was the one who had gotten her the apartment in Fargo. Got her to enroll in college. Insisted she "make something of herself."

When he finished his sandwich, he handed her half his chocolate chip cookie. He called out to his secretary to bring them both a cup of coffee. Lots of sugar and cream.

As Cash sipped her coffee, Wheaton finally spoke. "There's a body over at the hospital. In the basement. Looks to be about thirty, maybe thirty-five. Maybe Indian. Kinda hard to tell. She floated in with the floodwaters. Some high school students who drove to the edge of town to watch the water come in found her. Thought if you came and got a look at her you might be able to tell me something."

Years ago, when Cash was in junior high, she had checked out a book from the bookmobile about meditation and yoga. Books were her escape from the world she lived in. There were days in the foster home where she was forced to sit in a chair with no food for the weekend. Bathroom breaks were scheduled three times a day. With nothing better to do, she practiced reading the minds of the people in the house. When she got bored with that, she practiced out-of-body travel and bending metal forks with her mind. She had discovered that mind-reading wasn't that hard, and that the out-of-body experience involved slipping out of her physical body and traveling through the air.

There were nights she dreamt she was an eagle gliding through the sky, looking down through rooftops, seeing what people were up to. Through these dream experiences she often knew things would happen before they did in the physical world. Or she found out things she wasn't supposed to know. Her knowledge of one foster father having an affair with a woman from the church had caused untold drama when Cash had casually let it slip one evening over dinner, saying, "*I had this crazy dream.*" Everyone went berserk, with her taking the worst beating.

After that, the next time she saw Wheaton at a school basketball game, she went up into the bleachers and sat by him. When he'd asked how things were going, she told him the dream. She explained how everyone in the family had freaked out. She told him sometimes she knew things and then they would happen; they would come true. Wheaton just nodded and listened without comment. He was one person Cash could count on to not make her feel crazy.

A few months after that conversation, Cash dreamt about some boys from a neighboring town who stole a pickup and some gas from a farm way out in the country. She did not know Wheaton was looking for whoever was stealing gas and vehicles from farmsteads throughout the county. When she told Wheaton her dream, she was surprised by all the details of the dream he wanted to know. Cash had said, "All I dreamt was the ringleader's first name, and that he's from Felton." Within a week, Wheaton had found the ringleader and his wannabe gang members. The main kid was sent to some state juvenile facility. After that, Wheaton asked her to share any other dreams or hunches with him she might have from then on.

After the foster father's affair drama, Cash learned not to discuss what she knew with anyone except Wheaton.

"What do you think?" Wheaton's question pulled her back into the current situation.

"Beats school. Or hauling sandbags."

Wheaton stood and pulled on his winter coat. "Stay," he said to Gunner. "Mind if we walk? We can get there faster than it will take for the heater to kick on in the car."

Cash hadn't bothered to take off her winter gear. "Let's go then." Her voice was muffled from behind the scarf she rewrapped around her neck and over her mouth.

They walked in silence the short couple blocks to the county hospital. Wheaton led the way into the basement, which served as the county morgue. Their footsteps down the stairs and across the marble floor echoed. Cash got chills as they stepped inside the heavy door that opened into the morgue.

A body, covered with a white sheet, lay on a metal table in the middle of the room. The air smelled of formaldehyde and alcohol. Doc Felix sat on a metal stool pulled close to another metal table that was bolted to the concrete wall. Cash fought the urge to gag, not sure which repelled her more, the sight of Doc Felix or the sight of Doc Felix eating a chicken sandwich in the same room as a dead body.

In an earlier situation, she'd met Doc Felix when a dead man was found in a field northwest of town. At that time, Doc Felix's breath had smelled of alcohol, and his disrespect toward the dead man, who was from the Red Lake Reservation to the north, had angered her. She reckoned her feelings were justified by the way he had looked her up and down with distaste.

He turned to Wheaton. "S'pose you're here to see the waterlogged girl." He walked to the table and unceremoniously pulled the sheet down to the naked dead woman's waist. He smirked at Cash as he did so.

She ignored him. She looked at the woman. Her long brown hair lay in ropey strands.

Doc Felix walked around the table, inspecting the woman, side-eyeing Cash. "Kinda looks like you. Maybe a relative, huh? Then again, you all kind of look alike—hard to tell apart sometimes."

"Quiet, Doc," said Wheaton. "What do you know about cause of death?"

"She didn't drown. No water in her lungs. If I had to guess, she took a few hits to the head. And then she was most likely smothered." He pointed to some lumps that were just visible under her hair.

"Someone beat her to death?"

"I think she probably got knocked out. Then smothered to finish the job."

Cash kept silent while the men talked. She slowly walked around the table. Doc Felix was right; the woman could have passed for Cash's relative, but she doubted it. The woman was lighter-skinned than Cash's year-round tan. Although that might be because she had been in the water. She was too young to be Cash's mother and too old to be her sister, neither of whom Cash had seen in sixteen years. Cash shook her head, more to her own thoughts than to anything either man in the room was saying.

She caught a glimpse of a thick, tall dark shadow standing in the corner of the morgue. When she turned to look squarely at it, she heard a guttural *hmmph* and the shadow dissipated.

She looked back at Wheaton and Doc Felix, both of whom were standing and facing the direction the shadow had been in; neither showed any concern. Cash redid the scarf around her neck and tilted her head at Wheaton, signaling she was ready to leave.

As they started to walk away, Doc Felix asked, "Don't you want to know what I found in one of her garments?"

They both turned back around.

Felix was smirking. "Sorry I didn't say anything right away. Slipped my mind." He turned around and opened a drawer in the steel table against the wall. "Found this in her bra. All folded up and wet. Been letting it dry out. Looks like a page torn from a hymnal. One line's in English, the other in gibberish." He handed the damp piece of paper to Wheaton, who looked at it carefully before handing it to Cash.

Cash scanned the page. "*Asleep in Jesus! From which no one ever wakes to weep.*" The words of the song continued down the sheet between the musical notes. Underneath the English words were others written in Ojibwe, a language Cash would have known if she hadn't been separated from her family and raised in white foster homes.

An electric current ran from the paper to her hands, stinging her fingertips. She quickly handed it back to Wheaton and left the room. The swinging doors closed behind her with a swoosh. She was halfway up the stairs before Wheaton caught up with her.

THEY WERE SILENT ON THEIR walk back to the jail. Gunner's ears perked when they entered. Wheaton absent-mindedly scratched the dog's head as Cash took a seat on the bench. "How come you never answer your phone?"

"I don't know. I don't know how to use it."

"You just pick it up, say 'hi,' and talk with the person who is calling you."

"Seems strange to talk to someone who isn't there."

Wheaton's laugh was soft. "That's funny coming from you."

Cash leaned her elbows on her knees and looked at her feet, her long hair shading her face.

"Hey, hey. I was just teasing. How about this? When I call, I'll let it ring two times, then hang up, and call back, let it ring three times. If you don't answer the first time, I'll call again. Two rings, hang up, then three. That way you'll know it's me."

"Sure."

"And say goodbye before you hang up." He paused. "What'd you think about the woman there?"

Cash shook her head; another shiver ran down her back. "Just a bad sense about the whole thing."

"Indian?"

"Probably from White Earth way."

"That's what I thought too."

"Not much we can do with this water all around."

"Nah, take a couple of more days for it to reach the river and head north. I do think we've seen the worst of it. Once the roads east are clear, you could drive over and ask around?"

"Yeah. What am I asking around about?"

"Those towns at White Earth are small. Someone will know if someone is missing."

"Maybe she was married to some white guy, and he's the one who did her in?" Cash's mind went back to the creep Doc Felix.

"S'pose that's possible."

"How's Geno doing?" Cash shifted the subject. The dead man from Red Lake, who had been left in a field out by Halstad, a small town west of Ada, right smack on the Red River—that town was most likely buried in the floodwater today—had had seven children. The children were abandoned when their mother died from grief, although most folks blamed alcohol. Geno and his brothers and sisters had jumped Cash in the woods when she had gone to talk to the family about their father's death.

They had tied her up until she convinced them to untie her, partly with bribes of a cigarette. The group of seven grieving, distraught brothers and sisters thought she was going to turn them in to the social workers, who in turn would place them in foster homes. She did no such thing, but it ended up not making a difference in the end. When the other kids were placed in foster care or with an aunt, Geno had opted to hitchhike to Ada to try and find Cash. Instead, he found Wheaton, who had taken him in.

"He's in school. Still works as janitor on weekends here at the jail, but his real talent is art. I've been looking into this place down in New Mexico. An Indian art school."

"He wants to go?"

"Think so. Told him he can always come back here and push a broom if he doesn't like it. The kid lost his mom and dad. Came down here on his own. Doesn't seem to be afraid of change. Speaking of change, how is school going?"

"Fine." Before he could ask for any more details, Cash stood and headed for the door. "Gonna head back to Fargo. I'll watch the news and head over to the reservation as soon as the roads clear."

"If I get any word on who she is, I'll call. Two rings, hang up, three rings."

Cash gave him a farmer salute and headed out. She walked the few blocks to downtown and went into the first bar she saw. Smoke and the smell of stale beer greeted her, along with a blinking Hamm's beer bear sign. Al was sitting at the bar, a half-full glass of beer before him.

"Hey, Al, let's go. We can stop at the liquor store, and you can get you that twelve-pack I owe you."

Al drained his glass and slid off his stool. He pulled his leather workman's gloves out of his pockets and grinned. "Let's go."

Cash gave Al the money to get a twelve-pack for himself—his beer of choice—and a six-pack of Bud for her and waited outside the liquor store while he went in. Then, they each carried their own back to the boat, which still sat tied to the signpost. "Hope it don't rain," he said, looking at the clouds passing overhead.

"Nah." Cash hopped into the boat and rewrapped her scarf around her neck, this time low enough on her chin so she could still drink a beer. "Just better hope you don't get stopped for open bottle."

Al laughed as he climbed in. They used the oars to push out into the deeper water. He skillfully turned the boat around to head south, then stood to pull the rope to crank the outboard motor into gear. Cash held her beer tight between her knees and grabbed the sides of the boat to steady the rocking. When the motor kicked on, he steered into the deeper ditch water. "The water's already gone down a couple inches I think," he said.

"What kinda work you do?"

"Backyard mechanic. Cars and farm machinery."

The hum of the motor was the only sound breaking the silence as they rode south and drank beer. It was a cold ride made more so by a slight breeze coming off the freezing water. Too cold to enjoy the Marlboros Cash tried to smoke, she gave up on it, flicking it out into the water.

Once back in Moorhead, Cash helped Al get his boat hitched to his pickup, then hopped in the cab to ride back to his place where she had parked her Ranchero.

Al cranked up the heat and turned on a country western station. Hank Williams sang of folks fighting and drinking. Cash looked at Al with a side glance. He looked a bit older than her. The few beers he'd had didn't seem to have affected him. The sadness in his eyes looked familiar. It reminded her of her brother, Mo, who had recently re-upped for another tour in Vietnam. Unlike her brother, Al seemed calm, steady. "Were you in 'Nam?"

"Short time. Got a leg full of shrapnel."

Al skillfully backed the pickup truck into his yard, which was filled with spare auto parts, like he must have done it a hundred times. Not five inches between the garage and the small, worn house to spare. As he threw the pickup into park, he asked, "Wanna come in and finish your beer? Could heat us up a can of soup or something."

"Sure." Cash had never had a guy offer to cook her up something, and the only food she'd had all day was the half sandwich Wheaton had shared with her.

Inside his house, Cash sat at a small metal table in his kitchen, nursing her beer and smoking a Marlboro while he made vegetable beef soup from a can. They ate in silence while a country western singer crooned, and a female singer sang of moonlight and midnight walks.

When they finished eating, Al put the bowls in the sink and opened two beers, carrying them both into his living room. "Come on. Watch some TV?"

At first, Cash hesitated, almost said she needed to go home, but she changed her mind and followed him into the other room. She sat on a dark green couch covered in some '50s nubby fabric while he turned on the TV and adjusted the metal rabbit ears on top of the console to make the picture come in clearer. He switched channels until he found a station with a cop show about Marshall McCloud from New Mexico, who was working with the New York City police. Cash was content to watch. She sipped her beer and smoked the occasional cigarette. She didn't own a TV, and the Casbah bar tended to have their channel turned only to sports or the news.

During one scene where Marshall McCloud was explaining to the city police how to catch their bad guy, Al broke the silence between them. "This why you went to Ada? My friend told me you sometimes help the sheriff out—give him clues on how to catch the bad guys."

Cash shrugged and took a drink of her beer.

Al put his arm across her shoulders and pulled her close. "Live dangerously, do you?"

"Not at all."

"Not what I heard."

His kiss tasted of beer and cigarettes. It felt good to be held. He was a thin guy, not too tall, not too short, and their bodies fit easily on the couch.

When they finished having sex, they lay on the couch and smoked a cigarette. Al leaned over her every once in a while to get a drink from his beer sitting on the floor.

After a few minutes, Cash wiggled out from under him, sat up and pulled on her clothes. "Which way's your bathroom?"

He pointed to a hallway. "On the left."

When she came back into the living room, he had pulled his jeans on but was still laying down. He grabbed her hand and tried to pull her on top of him.

"Nah, I gotta get back to the other side of the river."

He let her go and sat up. "You sure?"

She picked her cigarettes off the floor and pulled her keys out of her back pocket. "Sure."

Cash's brain was silent as she drove across the bridge into Fargo toward the Casbah. The river had crested just a foot or two under the bridge.

As she walked in with her cue stick, Shorty slid two beers

in her direction. She put her quarters up and played until closing time—timing her beers so she didn't get too drunk. When her on-again, off-again married lover, Jim, suggested he stop up after closing, she shook his arm off her shoulder, said no, and went home alone.

The water didn't drop low enough for the roads to clear for three days. Cash went to her classes at the college. She used the typewriter in the American Indian Student Service's office to write her psychology term paper on Maslow's hierarchy of needs that she knew the professor wanted. She didn't write about growing up without enough food or parents. Or growing up in hostile environments, never knowing when the next move to another foster home would occur, nor living with people who made no secret of disliking her—no, outright hating her—she didn't write any of that. She didn't write about how she secretly questioned Maslow's hierarchy, as she thought she was doing pretty well for herself in spite of all that had happened to her. Nope, she wrote the paper the professor wanted, the paper that would get her an A, the one that extolled Maslow's theory and his brilliance.

When the essay was typed, she slid it under the professor's door. She had taken his class because it was the one psychology course that was graded on term paper and final test grade, not class attendance. She was learning how to get through college by attending the fewest classes possible. All of which gave her the education Wheaton wanted her to have while still giving her the free time she wanted to shoot pool in the rec hall, work the fields in season and hold her nightly spot at the pool tables at the Casbah.

By the third day of writing papers, playing pool and watching the water recede on her daily trips back and forth across the Red, Cash was going a little stir crazy. No rain or snow had fallen to add to the swollen river. Highway 75, which ran north and south, was finally clear to drive, which meant that roads to the east had to be clear also.

On the fourth day, she checked that her .22 was still behind the front seat of the Ranchero. The gun would come in handy if she hit a deer and needed to put it down mercifully. In the past, it had also come in handy to keep red-neck farmers at bay when they got a little too drunk and "handsy." She never traveled too far without it or the Thermos she filled with hot coffee. It took her forty-five minutes driving straight east to reach the eastern edge of the White Earth Reservation. She passed waterlogged fields along the way. It would take a good month before all the water that had traversed the valley either made it to the Red or would sink deeply into the ground.

The first place she stopped was the tribal police headquarters in the town of White Earth. A thin man wearing the tribal police officer uniform sat at a desk with a Zane Grey novel in his hands. *Must be a slow day on the rez.*

"What can I do for you?" the man asked, placing his thumb between the pages to save his spot.

"I'm from Norman County. Sheriff Wheaton asked me to come by. A woman floated into Ada with the flood. She's laying in the morgue over there. No ID."

"And who are you?"

"Cash . . . Renee Blackbear."

"Why is the sheriff sending a kid to ask questions?"

Cash stared at him. Brown eyes met brown eyes. He looked away first. "You can give Wheaton a call," she said.

"What does she look like?"

"Light skin. Long hair like mine but lighter brown. About my height and weight."

"Could be anyone from these parts. Haven't heard of anyone missing though." He peeked at a page in the book.

Cash turned to leave. She was annoyed at his disinterest. She felt angry that he appeared more interested in a book than a real-life situation.

"Anyone I should call if I hear anything?" he said to her back.

"Wheaton over in Ada."

When she reached the door, she looked over her shoulder at him. He was already reading from his book again.

Cash got back in her Ranchero and drove to the liquor store in Ogema. In rural areas, people who drove into town prolonged their time away from their isolated farms by gossiping to store clerks and bartenders. She figured the woman behind the counter would have heard if anyone was missing. The woman shook her head no. Cash bought a pack of cigarettes and left.

Next, she drove to the school at Pine Point on the southwest corner of the reservation. With no store, gas station, or bar, all life in the tiny village centered around the school, so it seemed the logical place to ask around. No one anywhere had any information about a missing woman. At each place, especially at Pine Point, folks had looked her over. She could read it in their eyes, "city Indian."

Cash's voice carried the inflection of the white families she had lived with and gone to school with. The people on the reservation talked with an accent flavored by the nasal sound found in the Ojibwe language. They dropped endings to words or shortened them. Bemidji became Bemidj. Other words were run together into one word. "I don't know" became "dntno." Body language oftentimes spoke louder than verbal language. A tilt of the head or a small point of the lips told whole stories if one knew how to read them.

Cash also carried her body like the farmers she had lived with, worked for. She strode with purpose. She stood with firm feet planted on the ground. Shoulders squared back, a ready-to-fight stance, from all the fights she had finished when taunted for being Indian.

The Indians on the reservation walked with more ease, their feet soft on the ground. They laughed and joked with one another, the women throwing their heads back with ruckus laughter, hands covering their mouths, their eyes sparkling. The lightness could disappear in a moment if a stranger entered the space. Eyes would drop downward, mirth gone in an instant.

These were all significant differences as Cash tried to garner information about the missing woman.

The last place she stopped was the Red Apple Café in the small town of Mahnomen on the western edge of the reservation. She asked the waitress, whose name tag said Debbi, the same question she had been asking all day. The answer was the same, no. As she finished off her hot roast beef sandwich, she thought to ask, "Where do folks go to church where they sing in both English and Ojibwe?"

"All the Episcopal churches do," answered Debbi, leaning forward on the counter, eager to finally be able to share some information. "But I heard there is another church, some kind of holy roller, speak-in-tongues kinda church, somewhere out west here on the prairie."

"You know where?"

"Nah, just heard it's out there on the prairie west of here. You could maybe ask at the church. The pastor probably knows where it is."

"Thanks." Cash finished her sandwich, drank her coffee and laid some bills on the table.

She drove slowly through town until she spied the small white church. A two-story parsonage, larger than the church, sat a few yards away. She tried the church door first. It was open, so she stuck her head in and hollered "hello." No answer. She went to knock on the parsonage door, which opened before she raised her arm. A white woman, wearing a flour-dusted apron, invited her in, waved her to a seat at the kitchen table covered with flour, a pan of rising bread dough and one loaf in the middle of being kneaded.

"What can I do for you, child? Reverend is out doing a visit. He'll be back shortly. Let me finish getting this loaf in the pan. Get yourself a cup of coffee. A bit chilly out there today. Thank God the floodwaters moved on. You related to the Jacksons? No? You sure do look like them. Fairbanks maybe? Go ahead, the coffeepot is on, the cups are up there in the cupboard. Help yourself. I would hate to have this bread fall—got Ladies Aid meeting tomorrow. Haven't seen you around here before."

Cash pushed the wooden chair away from the table and poured herself a cup.

"Cream's in the fridge, sugar on the counter there. What brings you to town? Maybe I can help."

"A woman's body washed in with the flood. The sheriff in Norman County thinks she might be from around here. Sent me to see if anyone has reported anyone missing."

"He sent a child? What kind of sheriff is he?" She slapped the loaf she was kneading on the table.

"I'm studying Criminal Justice at the college. I've helped him out before."

"I must be getting old; you look like you can't be a day over twelve. I haven't heard anything about anyone missing.

Mm-mmm-mmm. What is this world coming to? Is this woman alive?"

"No."

"Bless her soul."

"The waitress in town talked about a church west of here that some folks go to?"

"Oh my, if I was Catholic, I would cross myself. It's a fundamentalist branch. You do hear stories about their carrying on. You don't want to go there. No, siree. Why are you interested in them? Oh, dear lord. There's enough trouble around here with all the 'Who's better?' Christians? The Catholics or Lutherans? Us Episcopalians stay away from those conflicts." She laughed. "Don't need any holy rollers around here to mess things up more." She slapped the dough on the table even harder than before, sending white flour dust flying in Cash's direction.

"The woman had a page from a hymn book tucked in her . . ." Cash hesitated on saying the word "bra" to a reverend's wife. ". . . in her pocket. It was in both Ojibwe and English."

"I would stay away from them if I were you." The reverend's wife pointed her flour-covered finger at Cash. "Young girl like you. Nothing but trouble, them folks. Preying on the downtrodden, broken-hearted. And I hear that preacher might be up to some hanky-panky with vulnerable young women. You're not broken-hearted, are you? We can pray right here." She plopped down on a kitchen chair, hands folded on the table in front of her. A serious look in her eye.

"No. No," answered Cash quickly. "I'm just trying to find

anyone who might know who this woman is. If you tell me where the church is, I could just drive out there and ask."

"Would be sending you to the devil himself, my girl. No, no, no. Won't get that info out of me." The reverend's wife stood up and started beating another loaf of bread, flour flying over her and Cash.

Cash drank her coffee down and rinsed the cup out in the sink. As she moved toward the door, the reverend's wife called after her, "I'll pray for you, dear. You stay away from that place. Go back to your studies at the college. This community needs more college-educated folks. You take care, hear?"

Cash brushed flour dust off her jacket as she walked to her truck. Once inside, she sat with the truck idling in neutral, waiting for the heat to kick in. *What the heck was that all about?* she wondered. She backed out of the parsonage driveway and drove back to the Red Apple.

"Back for dessert, hon?"

"Nah, just wondering where that church is you told me about?"

"I'm not sure. Somewhere on some gravel road out toward Twin Valley."

Cash turned to leave.

"You better be careful driving out that way. Floodwater ran right through here, and I'm not sure all the roads are safe. Some of them washed out, I heard."

Cash headed south on the main highway outside of Mahnomen and then turned west on the first gravel road she came to. The waitress had been right. The road was washed out about five miles in—Cash had to turn back to the main highway. She tried the next turnoff. That road went a few miles farther. She drove slowly and scanned the horizon. She dropped her speed to a crawl. There to the north, probably right by the road that was washed away, Cash could see the steeple of an old country church.

She braked to a stop and got out of the truck. It was silent in the cold spring air. No birds yet. Not even the crows. Back in the distance, she could hear a car on the highway she had just turned off of. With few trees or buildings to buffer noise, sounds carried long distances on the prairie. Living in the Valley all her life, Cash could tell if a car was beyond five miles away or "just down the road." She could also distinguish the sound of car tires on pavement or gravel. And the difference between the sound of truck tires or car tires on either one. After the car on the pavement a few miles back had passed, Cash listened to the stillness of the prairie again while she stood looking toward the church. No way to get there. If she remembered correctly, that might be the church where she had seen graves for two small children last fall. Both having died around two years of age. Both in the same family plot.

Suddenly, Cash noticed a large dark figure moving away from the church, heading toward her. She didn't normally feel fear, but her chest tightened. She felt her heart start to pound in the veins of her neck and up into her ears. Everything in her body was screaming, *run!* She took a deep breath and screamed, "Fuck you," to the dark shape advancing across the field. Then she turned and jumped into the truck. She got it started as fast as she could and turned around in the mud ruts of the road. She felt the Ranchero almost slip into the ditch, but she corrected the front wheels, pulled forward and sped back to the highway, constantly checking her rearview mirror.

When she reached the highway, she threw the truck into park and stood on the floorboard near the driver's seat, not getting fully out of the truck. She looked over the cab in the direction she had just come from. She couldn't see the dark shape anymore. She shivered, and goosebumps ran up her back and down her arms. She slid back into the truck and turned the heater on full blast, then put the stick shift into gear and headed straight back to Fargo.

Cash didn't stop until she pulled into a parking spot in front of the Casbah. She grabbed her cue stick from behind the seat and made her way inside. Shorty passed two Buds across the bar to her when she entered. The place was filled with smoke and more folks than usual. The flood was bringing all the farmers into town; a place to bemoan the loss of livestock, haystacks or outbuildings. A place to brag about how close the water got to their houses and how the sandbags kept the river at bay. More than one cursed the lack of flood insurance.

Cash shot pool, drank beer and danced the occasional two-step with one drunk farmer or the other. It wasn't until closing time that she stepped out into the chill air and remembered the dark shape moving from the church, across the field, toward her. She looked up and down the sidewalk. Nothing.

Still, she got in her truck faster than normal and drove, on edge, the short distance back to her apartment.

Once inside, she turned on all the lights, even the dull bulb over the stove, and pulled the shades, which she never did. One of them zinged back up on its roller. The noise made her jump. She finally got it pulled down. She hung a towel over the window on the kitchen door and, just for the hell of it, another one over the mirror in the bathroom.

Most of the time she slept naked, but tonight she crawled into bed wearing her T-shirt and undies. Not completely satisfied, she got up, threw on her jeans and ran downstairs to grab her .22. Back upstairs, she checked to make sure it was loaded and laid it under her bed within arm's reach. She drank one more beer and smoked three more cigarettes before pulling the covers up and laying down under them.

At first she couldn't decide which direction to face to fall asleep. If she looked toward the bedroom window, she would be able to see if anyone tried to come in through it, although it would mean crawling straight up a brick wall. The only person she had ever known to do that was her brother, Mo, in a PTSD flashback right after he got back from the war. With that memory, she knew Mo was back in 'Nam and decided to turn and face the kitchen door. She would be ready if someone, or something, came through it. Feeling better about her decision, she fell asleep, her free arm hung over the edge of the bed, just in case she needed her .22.

Sunshine streamed through the cracks of the pull-down shades. She laughed at herself as she grabbed the .22 out from under her bed and leaned it in the corner by the kitchen door so she would remember to put it back in her truck. Cash removed the clothes she had slept in and threw on some others. She shook her head at her foolishness as she took the towel off the bathroom mirror. She made sure she had a pack of smokes, a full Thermos and headed across the river to school.

In spite of the sunshine, the temperature wasn't much above freezing. She attended the two classes that graded on attendance and took verbatim notes. Next, she went to her judo class, where she was finally able to throw the instructor over her shoulder. After class, she took a quick shower in the locker room before her drive to Ada.

When Cash entered the jail, Wheaton was behind his desk, Gunner at his feet.

"How's it going?" he asked. Gunner looked at her and then dropped his head on top of Wheaton's left foot.

"I drove over to White Earth. Asked around. No one knows anything. You hear anything?"

"No. Doc Felix still has the body."

Geno walked out of the cell area, a mop in one hand and a bucket in the other. He nodded hello to Cash. When she had first met Geno, he had been a kid with no meat on his bones. Now, thanks to Wheaton's cooking and steady living, the kid was filling out, although he was still pretty scrawny.

"No school today?" Cash asked Wheaton.

"Some kind of spring conferences. Kids get three days off."

"Why don't you lend him to me today? I'll drive back over by White Earth and check out this church people are talking about. Some kind of holy rollers. I got a feeling about them."

Geno was already putting the mop and bucket away in the utility closet.

"We should be back before dark." Cash stood and wrapped her scarf around her neck, then pulled on her mittens. "Dress warm, kid. Be mighty cold out there if I break down and you gotta push."

Wheaton laughed. Gunner looked up at Cash with a "why don't you just hurry up and leave" look. Cash bent down, rubbed his head and whispered, "I was here first, you little runt."

"What?" asked Wheaton.

"Just saying goodbye to the mutt."

Wheaton pulled a couple bills out of his billfold and handed them to Cash. "Feed the guy. He eats like a horse."

Cash and Geno left the jail and climbed into her Ranchero. On the way out of town, she filled up her tank—no way was she gonna run out of gas out by that freakin' church. She grabbed a couple candy bars and a bottle of pop for each of them, then headed east. Neither talked much on the way. Cash drove to Mahnomen and then backtracked south to the first gravel road turnoff.

She didn't like the feeling she got once she turned onto the gravel road. Geno seemed to get quieter too, although he hadn't said much of anything the whole ride. The water had cleared from the road, but there were still mud pits and some deep tire tracks where someone had gotten stuck; fortunately, her truck made it around them without getting bogged down. *Come on, baby*, she thought and patted the dash as they sloshed through another pit. The back end of the truck slid dangerously close to the ditch, but with a twist of the steering wheel, she was able to center it back on the road.

As the church came into view, Cash slowed and scanned the horizon. She felt Geno tense. "What was that?"

Cash looked to where Geno was pointing. She didn't see anything. "What?"

"Something just moved around the corner of the church. Stop."

Cash stopped and felt the truck sink a bit into the mud.

"What did you see?"

"Some great, big, dark thing. Like a guy, but not. Like dark air. Let's get out of here."

Cash put the truck into first and lifted her foot off the clutch. The truck eased forward.

"Nah, Cash, come on, let's go."

Just then, Cash saw the dark figure as it appeared then disappeared back around the corner of the church. She leaned forward over the steering wheel, trying to get a better look, even as everything in her body screamed for her to run.

"Cash, let's go. Come on."

The darkness lumbered menacingly toward them without seeming to make much headway.

Cash quickly put the truck in reverse to back down the

muddy road. Scared, she gave the truck too much gas and it fishtailed back and forth across the road, threatening to send them in the ditch once again.

"Slow down," Geno yelled at her.

Cash lifted her foot off the gas pedal. She sure as hell didn't want to get stuck out here. She worked the steering wheel left and right, willing the wheels of the truck to keep it on the road.

Geno was breathing hard. He would stare at the shadow approaching them, then look at the road behind them. They finally reached a spot on the road where the gravel was packed more solid and Cash was able to make a three way turn to get them headed in the right direction.

"Go. Go," yelled Geno, hitting the dash in front of him as Cash hit the gas. Now, he was looking over his left shoulder out the back window. She peered in the rearview mirror and saw the dark shadow fade in the distance.

Neither spoke again until they were sitting in a booth at the Red Apple. The waitress poured Cash a cup of hot coffee and gave Geno a bottle of Coke. Cash smoked. Geno motioned that he'd like one too. She gave it to him.

"What can I get you kids?" Debbi, the waitress, laid plastic-covered menus on the table in front of them. "The meatloaf is good today, and we have homemade apple pie." She leaned with one hand on her hip while holding the glass coffee carafe in her other hand. "Did you ever find out who that woman is that you were asking about the other day?"

Cash shook her head no. "I'll take the hot roast beef sandwich. And apple pie. Geno?"

"Hamburger. And pie."

Another couple came in and the waitress moved to wait on them.

"That was the biggest jiibay I've ever seen." Geno took a swig of his Coke.

Cash raised her eyebrow in a question.

"Jiibay. Ghost. Dead ghost."

"Dead ghost? What do you mean, dead ghost? What do you know about 'em?"

"Know to stay away."

"I think maybe the woman in the hospital basement in Ada went to that church, at least once. It's just a feeling I have. I saw that dark form when we went to look at her body. Didn't seem like Wheaton or the doc saw it, though."

"They wouldn't. Least not the doc. I don't think Wheaton sees things like that either."

"So, what's jib-aye?"

"Jiibay. You see them sometimes around death. Around fights. Sometimes when there is a lot of drinking going on. You don't want to mess with 'em."

"Wheaton asked me to try and find out who the woman is. I'm not afraid of a ghost," she lied.

"Maybe you should be."

They went silent as the waitress brought their food, and they dug in.

"You could get some medicine to protect you," Geno volunteered around a mouthful of french fries.

"Huh?"

"You know, Indian medicine. There are folks who can give you medicine to protect you. Then you could go out there."

"And where is this 'medicine'?"

"Well, you'd have to know who to talk to. Couple folks up at Red Lake could give it to you. But I can't go back there. They'd throw me in juvie for running away and then either send me to Red Wing reform school or some white farmer foster home."

They went back to eating. Halfway through his pie, Geno spoke again. "We're on White Earth, right?"

Cash nodded yes.

"There's an old woman, Jonesy, I think is what they call her. She lives around this way. Over by Pine Point, I think."

"How do you know all this?"

"I dunno. Everyone knows. If you grow up on the reservation."

"Can we just go ask this Jonesy for some of this 'Indian medicine'?"

Geno shrugged. "Can't hurt to ask. Probably bring her a pack of cigarettes. Some material she can use to make a quilt."

"Do you know where she lives?"

"No, but we can just ask around. Someone at Pine Point will know."

Cash lit a Marlboro. Geno motioned for one too. She gave

him one. "We probably can't do it tonight. It's gonna be dark soon, and I don't want to be driving around these mud pit roads in the dark. Last thing I need is to get stuck out here."

"We could ride over to Pine Point. Find out where she lives."

"I s'pose. But I ain't driving around the woods in the dark."

Geno laughed for the first time all day. "Thought you said you weren't afraid of ghosts?"

THE TOWN OF MAHNOMEN SAT on the historical banks of the ancient Lake Agassiz. It was from this higher land that the floodwaters flowed into the Red River Valley. Up and out of the flood zone, the ground was dryer the farther east they drove. It took them about almost an hour to drive from Mahnomen to Pine Point.

They drove the backwoods through Tamarack Forest and got to the small village while there was still light in the sky. Not really a town, it was just a cluster of HUD government houses with picture windows and siding painted various pastel shades. Wooden steps led to the white front door of each house. In the middle of the village was an older home, squat, short to the ground, with a single step leading to the front door. A single electric wire line ran to the roof of the house. An outhouse, an outdoor bathroom, sat out back.

"Pull up there," Geno said. "Let me go ask." He didn't wait for Cash to say yes. He hopped out of the truck as soon as she stopped on the gravel driveway and was immediately greeted by three dogs of no particular breed. One yapped loudly. Another growled, but only circled Geno's skinny legs. The third dog barked wildly while it ran back and forth between Geno and the house. The dogs didn't seem to faze him. The door opened a few inches as he approached. Cash couldn't tell if it was a man or woman who answered.

Cash watched them have a conversation. Then a short older man stepped out of the doorway and pointed up the road to the west, then gestured north. Geno was nodding as the man made a few more hand gestures that Cash didn't quite catch. The man turned and went back into his house, and Geno came back to the truck.

"She's got a place back in the woods. I think you're right; we'll have to come back tomorrow. When these old folks say, 'It's just around the corner,' they can mean anywhere from half an hour to an hour away. I don't have school for two more days, so I can come back with you tomorrow. Get an early start in case we get lost in the woods."

Cash shook her head yes. Neither spoke until they were almost to Ada. The sun set in brilliant oranges as they drove west into the Valley. They passed a pretty little church with a well-kept graveyard a few miles out of town. Both watched it carefully as they passed by.

"So, what's with this geebay thing?"

"Jiibay. And you don't talk about it."

"Why?"

"They can hear you. They think you want them to visit.

Don't talk about them. Don't even think about them." He turned the radio louder as a singer crooned about lost love. Geno rolled down the window and let cold air fill the cab. After a few miles, he rolled it up and turned the radio down a bit, then said, "Wheaton showed me this school down in Santa Fe, New Mexico, I think. An Indian art school. He sent some of my drawings down there. Guess it's where Indians go to get famous as artists."

"You want to go?"

Geno shrugged. Cash recognized the shrug. She herself brushed off things that were important to her. Too many dreams had been dashed. Too many hopes lost. If you didn't want something too much, it didn't hurt that much if you didn't get it.

Geno answered, looking out the window at empty fields rushing by, "If they want me. I'd come back up on break and stuff. Wheaton sneaks me up north about once a month, so I get to see my brothers and sisters that are still living up there. I go stand out by the playground when the school lets them out for recess." He paused, lost in thought. "I'd come back on holidays, and he said he'd make sure I still got to visit them."

"That'd be good then, right?"

"Yeah."

They rode in silence once again until they reached Wheaton's house. "I'll pick you up in the morning."

"If you come early enough, Wheaton will have breakfast." Geno grinned. "Bacon and eggs."

"Huh. I'll try."

The next morning, Cash arrived at 7:45. The smell of fried eggs and bacon greeted her as she entered Wheaton's house. Gunner was under the kitchen table and, as always, ignored Cash's arrival. Geno was wearing a plaid flannel shirt. His thermal undershirt was visible at the collar. Wheaton was flipping eggs. "You still like 'em over-easy?"

Cash nodded. "Looks good. Haven't had a breakfast like this since Mo went back to 'Nam."

"Geno says you're driving back over to Pine Point. Some lady might have a lead on the woman in the morgue?"

Geno looked at Cash behind Wheaton's back and shrugged.

"Yeah. That's the plan," answered Cash.

"Coffee's in the pot." Wheaton pointed at the stove.

"No one's come looking for her?"

"Not yet. Doc Felix says he's running out of room to keep her. I told him no one in the county has died this week, don't know how he can be running out of room."

"He's a creep. Remember, if I die, you take me to Fargo. Don't let him touch me—dead or alive." She wiped egg yolk off her plate with a slice of toast.

As soon as Cash and Geno finished their breakfast and drained their cups, they put on their coats and headed out. Just as quickly as Geno got into the truck, he hopped back out. "Hold on a sec." A couple of minutes later, he jogged back with a JCPenney bag that he threw on the seat between them. "I was going to give this fabric to my sister the next time I saw her, but I figured we could give it to Jonesy, and I'll just get another yard before I visit them next time. I figured you got the cigarettes."

They rode in easy silence on the way back to the reservation. About halfway there, Geno said, "I didn't tell him about the jiibay. Didn't want him to worry."

Cash nodded that she heard him. Both watched the fields outside the truck windows. Each made an occasional comment about the water still standing in low spots. They watched wisps of white clouds pass overhead. Cash said, "At least those aren't rain clouds."

Geno pointed, without speaking, at a pair of robins hopping in a field. Between those small interactions, they rode the rest of the way listening to country music, while smoking Cash's cigarettes. They stopped once at a gas station to fuel up and get more cigarettes, pop and candy bars. "Cash, your tire is low."

Cash walked around to Geno's side of the truck. Damn, he was right. It wasn't flat, but it was low. "I'll pull up by the hose."

With gas in the tank, air in the tires and some candy bars for nutrition, they headed out. Geno told Cash she'd have to drive into the village of Pine Point so he could recall the directions the guy had given him yesterday. Once they were in front of the house they had stopped at the day before, he started giving her directions. *Go there. Turn here. See that yellow cloth tied on the fence post up there? Take a left at the next road.* Then another turn where a fallen pine tree was.

To Cash, it seemed like they drove for hours. Some of the

back roads were still soggy from the winter thaw. Others, especially farther into the woods, were still frozen solid. Eventually, they were on what she would call a hunting road, a straight lane that went deeper and deeper into the pine forest. She rolled down her window some to blow out the smoke from her cigarette when she caught a whiff of wood-smoke. "You smell that?"

Geno rolled down his window. "Yeah. We must be on the right road."

"What? You thought we weren't?"

Geno grinned. He tilted his hand back and forth in the sign of maybe, maybe not.

"There. Right there." Geno pointed across the dash of the cab. Set back, right off the road, was a very small, weather-worn log cabin. Cash would have missed it if Geno hadn't pointed it out. There was a short turn-in, snow was still in the ruts. She had to back up a bit to turn in.

Cash shut off the ignition. Neither of them moved. There was a stillness and absolute quiet—if there was a breeze or wind outside this forest, it wasn't moving anything this far in the woods. The spring birds hadn't returned yet. The smoke from the chimney of the cabin drifted soundlessly skyward. There was a woodpile to the side of the house—depleted from a winter's use, but still plenty for the remainder of the cold spring. An ax stuck out of the cutting log.

Cash hated to open the car door. The creaking and subsequent shutting of it would break the silence. She looked over at Geno, and he nodded in agreement. They both opened their doors at once, stepped out and shut them simultaneously. They walked in step to the front of the cabin—Geno with the JCPenney bag in his hands.

Before they got close enough to knock, the door opened and a woman of indeterminate age said, "I was waiting. Biindigen. Come on in." She was wearing men's denim jeans and two pullover sweaters. She gestured to the table where some saltine crackers and a bowl of popped wild rice sat. "Sit." She moved to a woodstove, grabbed a battered stainless steel coffee pot and poured two cups of tea for them. The tea smelled of cedar and some other scent Cash couldn't place. Then the woman sat down and set a mismatched china plate in front of each of them. She pointed at the food. "You must be hungry. It's a long drive back in here."

Cash was nervous. There was something about the woman that made her feel like a little kid. Cash took a couple crackers and, following Geno's lead, spooned some popped rice onto her plate. They ate it with their fingers. *How did she know we were coming? She had food and two plates and cups ready.*

"I pay attention. You pay close enough attention you know things ahead of time. You know how that is, don't you?" The woman looked directly into Cash's eyes. Cash immediately lowered her gaze to the food on her plate. "It's good that you came here first."

Geno put the JCPenney bag on the table. He looked steadily at Cash. Pointed with his lips to her cigarettes. She reached into her jacket pocket and rested an unopened pack on the bag. Geno slid it across the table to the woman, who

put a hand on top of the gifts and kept it there for a good minute. She nodded her head yes.

"Eat. So, I guess you know folks call me Jonesy. And you two are?"

"Geno."

"Cash."

"Your folks were from Red Lake, eh? And where you from, Cash?"

Geno hadn't said anything. How did she know where he was from?

"Your folks were from around here, eh?"

"Yes." Cash looked around. *Didn't see any telephone. Maybe the guy from Pine Point had driven out here and told her to expect them.*

Jonesy brushed dark bangs back from her forehead. "No. Like I said, sometimes you just know. It's okay. Nothing to be afraid of here. But you two had a scare yesterday, eh?" She put her hand back on the pack of cigarettes and cloth.

Cash could hear the crackers she was chewing. She looked at Geno. He lifted his eyebrows and gave a slight nod, saying with his eyes, *Everything's fine.*

Cash knew that she herself had a sixth sense, a word she had learned from library books. The knowledge helped her come to terms with the fact that, sometimes, she knew things, like the Johnson barn was going to catch fire, or that her foster sister was pregnant before anyone else knew. Wheaton knew she knew things. Which is why he had her help him out sometimes. She didn't think he understood exactly how she knew what she knew, but he trusted her knowing.

Jonesy got up and refilled their cups. "Good thing you came for a visit." Again, she looked directly into Cash's eyes. "You're gonna be okay. May not seem like it, but you will." She walked over to the double bed that sat against one wall. She got down on her knees, her back to them, and pulled out a cardboard box. Cash and Geno watched her lift things out of the box, then put things back in. She pulled out another box and rifled through it.

Finally, she pushed herself to stand, brushed off the knees of her jeans and came back to the table. Both Geno and Cash pretended they hadn't been watching her the whole time. She handed Cash a very small, green cloth pouch, the color of spring leaves. Cash could feel crushed leaves or some other dried plant through the fabric. It was tied with a long drawstring. "This is Indian tobacco. Put some out once in a while, give thanks for that gift you have."

Cash continued holding the pouch.

"Soon, the birds will be back. My house around here will be filled with them singing and carrying on." Jonesy paused. "Anyone ever asked you if you drink too much?"

Cash just looked down at the table.

"None of my business. Keep the pouch in your glove box. Put some tobacco out when you're gonna take off some place. You'll be fine."

Jonesy said some words in Ojibwe to Geno. He shook his head no. She said some more in Ojibwe. He looked at his plate, then back at the woman. He shook his head yes. He said a word Cash didn't understand.

"Good," Jonesy said. She crossed the room and dug through the boxes once again. When she came back, she handed Geno a small buckskin pouch.

The air in the room changed. It was a subtle change that Cash felt physically. Like her skin tightened on her bones after a hard workout. It was like things in the room took on a more solid form. Jonesy changed her demeanor also. She chatted with them like they were regular visitors from the village who had just stopped by for a cup of tea. Geno told her about his mom and dad passing. How he had hitchhiked to Ada to find Cash, but found Wheaton instead. And maybe he was going to art school. Jonesy told him that was a good idea, then asked Cash what she was studying and if she had a boyfriend. Cash was embarrassed. She knew Jonesy could figure that out without Cash saying anything, and neither Wheaton nor Geno knew anything about the men in her life.

Instead of answering, Cash said, "We should head back."

Jonesy laughed.

Cash pointedly looked at Geno's cup, signaling for him to finish it. She stood up, buttoned up her jacket and wrapped her scarf around her neck. Jonesy followed them to her door.

Cash walked out, got about three feet, then turned back. "Thanks," she said, touching the pouch in her jacket pocket.

"Sure thing. You come back and visit."

When Cash got to the truck, Jonesy called, "Don't go

back there today. You gotta get that tire fixed before you go running around the country." She turned and shut the door.

"Is that tire flat?" Cash was worried again.

Geno kicked the tire. "Nah, it's good. We can stop and check it again first gas station we see."

Halfway to Ada, they stopped and put more air in the tire. The sky was getting dark by the time Cash dropped Geno at Wheaton's. She didn't go in to say hi, just waved at Wheaton standing in the doorway, Gunner at his side. She drove straight to her apartment and fell into bed. Without her nightly beer or a last smoke.

THE FIRST THING CASH DID the next morning was look for the green pouch. It lay on top of her dresser. Cash picked it up. Felt it. Rubbed it between two fingers and listened to the rustle of the plant it held. She put the pouch in her jacket pocket. Then she washed up, got dressed and sat at her table to drink a cup of coffee.

She aimlessly played a game of solitaire with the cards her brother had left behind, while running the previous day over in her mind. Living in foster homes with little to no connection with other Native people, Cash wasn't sure if other people could sense and see things, things she'd practiced and gotten good at. Jonesy had answered questions that Cash was only asking in her mind. This ability to hear other people's thoughts was new to Cash. *How did Jonesy know what I was thinking?* She wondered if it was a skill she could develop herself. Then there was the conversation Jonesy and Geno had had in Ojibwe. Cash was going to have to remember to ask Geno what they said to each other.

With enough coffee and a couple pieces of toast in her belly, Cash put on her winter layers. Her plan was to drive east in the direction of Mahnomen and try and find the church again. She hopped in the Ranchero, and as she backed out of her parking spot, she felt a familiar thump, thump, thump. Her breath became bursts of cold clouds floating in the air as soon as she exited and walked around the vehicle. The tire was flat. She climbed back into the truck where the heater was running. *Damn.* She didn't have a spare.

Some things she was good at, as good as any man. Driving truck, doing fieldwork, hauling hay bales. She was a darn good shot with the .22. She changed her own oil—that was easy. Everyone in farm country knew how to change oil on a vehicle or machinery, but changing tires was one thing she had balked at learning how to do. It was a job better left to the men, who were always eager to give her a hand.

She finally shut off the engine and walked to the Casbah.

"I thought I told you I wasn't going to serve you anymore in the morning," were the first words out of Shorty's mouth.

"Just for that, give me beer."

When he hesitated, she halfway grinned. "I was kidding. I have a flat. I need some help getting it changed. Know anyone that can help?"

"I can help you with anything you need, doll." Ol' Man

Willie appeared to be nursing his first beer of the morning. He sat on a barstool instead of his spot in the back booth that he eventually ended up in each night. Back in the corner, he would be slouched over, the stench of piss making folks steer a clear path around him.

Cash leaned over the bar to Shorty. "Tell him to shuttup."

Shorty looked from her to Willie. Shook his head. "Where's your truck at?"

"Front of my apartment."

Shorty pulled the rotary phone out from under the bar. Set it on the counter. Dialed some numbers with his pointer finger—the phone clacking with each digit. She could hear the phone ringing and a man's voice say, "Hello?"

"Hey, Shorty here. Remember that girl who needed a boat ride up to Ada? Well, her truck has a flat. Wondering if you could give her a hand." He wiped the counter with his rag, even though it wasn't dirty. "Just down the street here. Out in front of the appliance store." He raised his eyebrows, silently asking Cash if that was where it was. She nodded yes. "Yep, out front. A Ranchero . . . No, no spare. Maybe take it off and see if it has a nail, maybe it can be patched if it's just a slow leak? Otherwise, she'll need a new tire . . . I don't know. You'll have to take a look when you get here." He said goodbye and hung up the phone.

"He'll be by in about a half-hour. You can get some practice in. Wanna pop?"

"Coke." She went and dropped four quarters in the pool table. Willie had spun the barstool around and was now leaning back on the bar with his elbows, his pelvis thrust in her direction.

"Shorty!"

"Come on, Willie. Leave the kid alone."

Willie slowly turned back to the bar.

Cash and Willie were the bar's only customers, and she was the lone player at the pool table. She played against herself, stripes against solids. When she got bored with that, she switched to practicing her cut shots. Then bank shots. "Shorty. What's taking him so long?"

Before he could answer, a guy wearing a Standard Oil uniform entered and looked around.

"Hey, Hank," called Shorty. "That's Cash over there. Her truck."

"Got the tire changed. It had a worn spot. Needed a new one."

"How much that gonna run me?" Cash was bent over the pool table, making a long shot.

"I got a deal. Ran over to Moorhead and picked up a good used one. Al said don't worry about it."

Cash stood up. Looked at him. Hank shrugged.

"What'd I owe you for labor?"

"A morning beer? Got me out of the shop for a couple hours. You probably need new tires all the way around at some point. Al said he could probably scrounge up three more."

"What are you drinking?"

"Beer. Wanna shoot a game? One quick game and a drink before I head back?"

"Rack 'em up." Cash walked over and asked Shorty for another Coke and a beer. She handed the beer to Hank. "One game, then I gotta go."

They played a slow game. Hank paced his beer to last until Cash dropped the 8-ball. Then he bought a pack of Juicy Fruit from Shorty and left. Cash put away the bar cues and waved goodbye as she headed out the door.

Back in front of her apartment, Cash walked around the Ranchero a couple times, inspecting all the tires. The new one was a different brand, had a bit more tread than the other three, but they looked good. She drove to her last classes of the day, then headed to Ada afterward.

It was getting on in the afternoon when she picked up Geno and drove east to Mahnomen. Geno said he wasn't scared anymore. "Just go ahead and drive on out to the church," he said. So she did.

No dark creature ventured out to greet them. And no one was in the church, although there were tire tracks in the parking lot. The front door was open, so they walked in. It was a modest church. Maybe twenty pews on either side of the aisle. A life-sized Christ on the Cross was behind the altar. Each pew had five well-worn red hymnals. Cash picked one up and flipped through the pages. She stopped, and went back and opened it to the table of contents, ran her finger down the list of hymns. "Asleep in Jesus," page thirty-two. Cash turned to the page. There was the hymn the woman had tucked in her bra. The Ojibwe words written below the English.

"Hey, Geno. Can you read this?"

He looked over her shoulder. "Nah."

"You understood Jonesy."

"I understand it when folks talk to me. I don't know how to read it."

"What did she say to you?"

"Who?"

"Jonesy."

"Asked if you and I were related."

"That's it?"

"And what my Indian name is."

Cash closed the hymnal and put it back. As she turned to leave the building, she saw a small stack of papers on a lectern they had passed. She picked one up and saw the name Pastor John Steene. Lillian Steene was the organist. Cash grabbed Geno's arm. "Come on. Let me show you something."

She scanned the graveyard as she walked toward it. The pine trees that circled it were silent. No wind blew through them. No birds sat in the branches. No dark figure stood guard. She reached graves close to the church and showed Geno the headstones—one for a Pastor John Steene stood next to one for a Lillian Steene. Their dates of birth were followed by unblemished granite waiting for dates of death. Cash pointed at the two other headstones in the family plot. They were small graves, all with the last name Steene. Then she pointed at the small barren grave with no headstone. "What do you see?"

"Looks like the kids died two years apart. Maybe they got some kind of family disease. Or the flu?"

"If it was the flu, they would've all kicked over at the same time."

"You're right there. Come on, let's go. I don't like graveyards."

Cash felt bad. She had forgotten the trauma Geno had been through recently. "Aw, sorry, let's go get some food. You can visit your favorite waitress."

"Wonder where Shadow Man was today?" said Geno.

"Who cares? I'm glad the old jiibay was napping."

Both let out a nervous laugh and looked at the graveyard behind them as they drove away.

At the Red Apple, they slid into a booth, and Debbi brought them each a cup of coffee. "My new best customers. What are you having today?"

Together they answered, "Same as last time."

"Hot roast beef for you and hamburger for you," she said, not bothering to write the order down.

Geno flipped through the songs on the small jukebox on the wall in the booth. Cash slid him some coins. Soon, Elvis was singing about suspicious minds. When Debbi came with their food, Cash held up the church program and asked her if she knew where this Pastor Steene lived.

"Gosh, I don't know. We don't see much of them folks around town here. Think they live on a homestead out by the church. But I don't know. We got a good Episcopal church right here in town. You don't need to get involved with them." She leaned down and, in a loud whisper, said, "Folks say they do some strange things out there. Speak in tongues

and roll in the aisles. I wouldn't go near there if it were me."
She gave both Cash and Geno a warning look.

Cash folded the program and stuck it back in her pocket.
"Don't plan on that. Just trying to get a lead on who the
woman might be in Ada."

"Still haven't found out who she is, huh? Well, If I hear
anything I'll be sure to let you know."

CASH AND GENO DROVE BACK to Ada. When she dropped
Geno off, she told him to let Wheaton know they still didn't
have a name for the woman, then drove back to Fargo. She
circled her truck and checked the tires before going up to her
apartment and putting the green pouch in the top drawer of
her dresser. She brushed her hair and braided it in two long
braids down her back. Then she headed to the Casbah.

Since the flood had receded, the Casbah crowd was back
to the usual folks. Ole and his brother, Carl, were back at the
bar, taking bets on whether Cash's long hair would get caught
in the screen door as it slammed shut behind her when she
entered. They then had running side bets on who was winning at the pool tables. Ol' Man Willie was in his booth by
the back door, periodically snoozing and sipping. The usual
farmers were there drinking, shooting pool. Some with their
wives or girlfriends. They all knew and tolerated one another.
It was a mellow night.

Cash spent Saturday reading her class assignments for the
next week. Her American Indian studies class assignment

was to read sections from *Bury My Heart at Wounded Knee* by Dee Brown. It was one of the classes where some of the grade was counted on attendance. In last week's class, two of the other Native students had turned the whole class into a giggling mess when the teacher, in all seriousness, wrote on the chalkboard and proclaimed, "Today, we are going to cover the Indian Non-Intercourse Act, better known as the Indian Intercourse Act. Who is ready to discuss the Indian Intercourse Act?"

From the back of the room, in a stage whisper, someone had asked, "Tezhi, did you and Bunk study the Indian Inter-course Act this weekend?" That comment had gotten the giggles going. The teacher never regained control of the class as more jokes were tossed about the room, more explanations given, all with undertones of sexual suggestion. The teacher finally ended class early after informing them the Indian Intercourse Act would be on the final exam. The students, Indian and white, had exited, all laughing.

Finished with her assignments, Cash swept the floors and pushed the dirt out the door. She gave the top step a quick sweep. The dirt flew to the ground below. Then she bagged her laundry and hauled it down the block to the laundromat. Once she washed, dried and folded it, she left it sitting on her bed. Life in foster homes demanded that Cash clean whole houses on a Saturday morning while dealing with all the family laundry. The habit was hard to break, although her definition of clean and a foster mother's definition of clean were opposing ideas.

By early afternoon, all her studies and housework were done. Again, out of habit from years working on farms, she hopped in her Ranchero and took a lazy drive the thirty-five miles north to Halstad on the Minnesota side of the river to check on the fields. Which ones were drying out from the flood. Which might be ready to plow or plant in the coming weeks. Farmers driving to Fargo tapped the brim of their hats in a friendly hello as they passed. From the road, she could see the branches of the trees that snaked along the river. They were thickening, which meant their leaves were almost ready to pop out. In a couple weeks, the dark branches would be springtime green.

While the flood had taken a toll, it wasn't catastrophic the way some floods in the Valley were. Cash didn't remember the last big flood. It had happened when she was still a toddler. She just remembered stories of cattle being rescued as they drifted north in the waters, and of houses buried to the chimney. This flood had covered the valley and moved on. The biggest casualty seemed to be the woman lying in the hospital basement.

As Cash drove, she cracked the side window open to pull the smoke from the cab of the Ranchero. Her mind drifted to the woman the flood had brought to town. Cash wondered how the woman had met foul play. Doc Felix had said she died before going in the water. Cash then remembered the image of the dark shadow coming at her in the hospital's basement and then across the field from the church. Her intuition told her this woman had met trouble somewhere other than the church, even if she had been attending services there.

Cash reached Halstad and crossed the river bridge northwest of town. The water below was reddish mud, the current swift. She turned south on the North Dakota side and drove slowly back to Fargo, again looking at the fields, at the gray clouds moving in from the west. She hoped it would rain, not snow. Although it certainly had been known to keep snowing even after the first spring thaw in this part of the country.

Back in Fargo, in the safety of her apartment, she put away her laundry—clean shirts and jeans on the chair in the bedroom, socks and undies in the top drawer of the dresser that sat next to her bed—then counted her pool winnings that she kept in a sock in the top drawer. Good, she had enough for this month's rent. She ran a brush through her long hair, rebraided it and headed to the Casbah for another night of beer, pool and country two-stepping.

At closing time, Jim wrapped his arms around her. "I need me some, Cash," he whispered against her neck.

"Go home to your wife, Jim. I gotta study." Cash slipped out from under his arm and went home alone.

The next morning Cash woke early. It was Sunday, and she was determined to go to church. She sifted through the pile of clean clothes and chose a cotton blouse, which was the closest thing she had to dress-up clothes. Cash didn't own a dress or a pair of dress slacks. She figured God probably didn't mind what she wore, so the church folks shouldn't either. Fully dressed, she dug around in her top drawer, grabbed some cash without counting it and stuck it in her pocket. She looked in the mirror over the bathroom sink and laughed at her reflection. She felt around in the medicine cabinet over the sink and found four bobby pins. She rolled her hair into a bun at the back of her neck and stuck the pins in haphazardly. It would have to do. Almost to the bottom of the stairs, she turned around, went back up and got the green pouch to put into the glove box.

The bulletin had said the first service was at 10 A.M. It was only eight o'clock when she left, so she made a quick swing by Wheaton's to try to get Geno to come along for the ride. He shook his head no. No church for him. Gunner gave her his "get out of here" look that she ignored.

Wheaton was frying up some eggs and bacon when he asked what she was doing all dolled up. When she told him, he raised an eyebrow. She informed him about stopping at the church and looking at one of the hymnals. The songs were in Ojibwe and English. Thought she should check it out.

Wheaton fed her an egg over easy and two slices of bacon. She was done in plenty of time to make the drive to the country church.

It was a sunny day. Most of the ditches still had water sitting in them, but not running through the culverts like before. It was slowly sinking into the ground around pale orange grass stubble. She could see a few cars sitting in the parking lot a good two miles out from the church across the flat prairie. No dark shadow appeared. She pulled in behind a wood-paneled family station wagon.

She lit a cigarette, cracked the side window and smoked while she watched men and women—some as families, some as individuals, enter the church. Most of the congregation appeared to be white, but there was a handful who were clearly Indian. The majority of the women wore dresses below the knees with high heels that sank into the water-logged earth in the churchyard, but some of the younger women wore dress pants. Cash then focused her attention on a group of three young men, who looked to be farmers, standing to the side of the church, having a smoke. Everyone outside was huddled in small groups against the spring chill.

The church bells rang. Cash jumped, startled. She hadn't expected that sound. The three smokers tamped their ciga-rette butts out into the ground with the heels of their shoes and headed inside. *Now or never*, thought Cash. She tossed her cigarette butt out and stepped on it on her way to the church door.

Inside, organ music was playing. Everyone was sitting except two ushers, who had just been outside smoking. One handed Cash a bulletin. She looked up and down the rows of congregants. In that glance, she estimated maybe thirty people at most, including children. Men on one side of the church. Women on the other. There was an empty row on the women's side. The other back pew had the third smoker, his long legs stretched out in front of him.

Cash guessed that six of the women in the congregation were Native. None of the men looked to be so. Suddenly, the organist switched the tempo of the hymn she had been playing into a fast rhythm. From a side door up by the pulpit, out stepped a man wearing a white robe with a purple stole draped over his shoulders and down his chest. An embroidered gold cross adorned each side of the stole.

There were no other words to describe him except tall, dark and handsome. Not dark like Indians are dark, but in the way white men can be described as dark and sexy. His deep brown hair was brushed back in a full sweep, with strands that slipped over his forehead—a John Kennedy kind of haircut. The pointed tips of his shiny black polished shoes peeked out from under his pastor robes. He entered, singing in a deep baritone, and motioned for the congregation to stand. They stood and belted out the hymn, sopranos and altos singing harmony, the men's voices not as exuberant as the women's. Cash stood with the crowd to get a better view of the goings-on.

The entire congregation swayed from left to right. The organist played like she was in a rock-and-roll band. As the music rose and fell, some of the congregants raised their hands above their heads, palms skyward. The organist stretched out the notes of the song, dampened the sound, but kept the rhythm going, kept the congregates swaying, as the pastor began a vibrant prayer for the sins they were all guilty of. He prayed to God to wash them in the River Jordan, save their heathen souls.

Cash had never witnessed anything like it. Lutheran churches in the Valley never celebrated God like this. The music and the prayers continued throughout the service.

The preacher preached. The congregants were fueled into spiritual rapture. He called them forward to be witness to Christ. To be blessed in His name. First to go forward were the older women of the church. Then a smattering of the men. The music swelled, the furor built, and the young women streamed forward.

In the back pew, Cash sat entranced. She recalled a time in grade school, might have been second grade, when she was in the children's church choir. They rehearsed and prepared a slow hymn to sing from the front of the church. Cash found the song and slow tempo all mighty boring. She had heard rock-and-roll songs on her older foster sister's transistor radio and loved the faster, jazzed-up tempo. That Sunday morning, as she stood in front of the congregation, Cash decided to liven up the song. She raised her voice, speeded up the tempo and swished the skirt of her dress around her hips. She felt proud of what she had done. Livened it up for folks, many of whom were smiling and laughing behind gloved hands held over their mouths. Hell was paid once the foster mother got her home, out of the public eye.

The look on the faces of the young women, who streamed to the altar for hands on healing, reminded Cash of her hippie friend Sharon. At the beginning of the school year, when Cash first met her, Sharon had been infatuated with their science teacher. Sharon's eyes would glaze over when she talked about him, unaware that her chest would rise up and push out her breasts.

The intensity of the sermon lasted all morning. The final

prayer ended with the pastor calling out first to the men's side of the church, and lastly, more fervently, to the women's side—*Any congregant who wants to . . . no, needs to, needs to lift the burden of sins off your conscience. Anyone, dear sisters, each and every one of you, are welcome to come to a prayer session, a healing session within the privacy of the church or in our home. Reach out and be healed. Feel the glory of God wash over you.*

If Cash were the praying kind, or maybe even the feeling guilty kind, she could have been swayed by the sermon and the pastor's good looks to go for a healing session herself. At the end of the service, the pastor strode down the aisle and the congregants followed him out, front row first. Cash had time to think about when she was just a kid. One of her foster mothers had beaten her black and blue for being a show-off. Cash had won top student award for the school, but she was accused of cheating and buttering up to the teachers to make them feel sorry for the *poor little foster kid*. Her foster mother had beaten her until she admitted she had indeed cheated and buttered up to the teacher, even though she hadn't. Anything to stop the striking. During the beating, the foster mother had also screamed that Cash was a heathen, a dirty, filthy Indian, guilty of all kinds of sins and was going to go to hell.

The coldness of the hardwood floor had eased some of the pain as Cash lay on her bedroom floor that night, vowing to herself to always tell the truth, no matter how bad the beating. She had quickly realized it didn't seem to matter whether she lied or told the truth; she was going to get beat. She had also vowed that night to never feel guilty for any choice she made in life. Like the times when she had no choice but to steal food because a foster family withheld food as punishment. Or the time when one of the teachers had given her a box of valentines to sign and give out to the class because the foster family hadn't given her any to hand out. The teachers at school were nice to her because she was smart, did her homework, was curious about the subjects they taught.

As she got older, sometimes she stole money from the foster homes to buy simple necessities like sanitary products or took aspirin from the bathroom cabinet she wasn't supposed to go into. Nope, those early beatings had taught her that she was doing nothing to feel guilty about. Her mind was her mind. Her choices were her choices, and she was fully capable and willing to be responsible to and for herself.

Sitting in church through the service had triggered all the foster care memories that continued to run through Cash's mind as she watched the people file out after the pastor. The line slowed as they stopped to shake his hand. His wife stood with gloved hands folded in front, at her waistline. Her smile didn't reach her eyes, and she shook no one's hand. Some she would give a slight nod to. When the pastor pulled some of the women—the shy ones—in for an embrace, Cash noticed that his wife's face tightened, and she leaned her hip against her husband's side. The adoring women noticed nothing.

Cash determined ahead of time she would shake his hand and keep moving, but when she got to him, he grasped her hand with both of his and said, "Dear child, you are new to our flock. Welcome. All are welcome here." His eyes never left Cash's. Mesmerizing. It felt like he was willing her to belong, to join, to become one of them. Cash felt his hand become hot as he grasped hers. She pulled away and looked at his wife. Cash put a hand out to her, trying to force his wife to move, breathe, do anything but stand there like a statue. Instead, his wife placed her hand on her husband's arm, looked seductively up at him, and then looked steely-eyed back at Cash.

In that moment, while looking between their shoulders, Cash saw the dark form in the graveyard. She dropped her hand and ignored the wife's gesture that finally reached out to her. Cash backed away, then walked rapidly to the Ranchero. The pastor was quick behind her. He grabbed her by the elbow, still smiling, still radiating, and said, "Don't run away from God. Stay. The women have a chicken dinner ready for us in the basement of the church."

"I gotta go." She jerked her arm away, then got in her truck, backed out and headed to Mahnomen. When she checked her rearview mirror, the darkness was gone. No one else had gotten in their cars and driven away. Cash pulled off to the side of the gravel road, held tightly to the steering wheel before getting out a cigarette and lighting up. She felt her heart beating in her chest with every inhale. Once done, she snuffed the finished cigarette out in the ashtray, put the truck in gear and continued the drive to Mahnomen, the gravel road crunching under the truck tires.

She drove at a farmer's pace toward Main Street. It was

empty. Not a car in sight. A cardboard clock with black hands read eight o'clock, but the sign right above it read CLOSED. Damn, she had forgotten that all these small towns closed up shop on Sunday. As she reached the northern end of town, she slowed to a crawl in front of the Episcopal church. That's where the town was gathered. The parking lot overflowed with some cars parked up on the shoulder of the road. Folks milled around in the parking lot. Men smoked. Kids chased one another around the church. The women, huddled in wool coats, chatted in groups of three or four.

Just as Cash got ready to make a U-turn and head back south, a woman walking to her car in the parking lot caught her eye. Their eyes met with recognition. It was Debbi, the waitress from the Red Apple. Dressed in her Sunday best. She motioned with a black-gloved hand, not a wave but a "hold on a sec" motion. Cash coasted to a stop on the side of the road, rolled down her window and waited for the woman to approach.

"Hey. Good morning. I almost didn't recognize you with your hair up."

Cash self-consciously touched her hair. "Morning."

"The café's not open today."

"I saw."

"Did you hear the news about the other woman?" Debbi lowered her voice and looked around, as if afraid someone might overhear.

"No."

"It's not the one you were asking about. Some guy out

checking his trapline found this one over by Little Lake. Indian girl. You said the other one is Indian too?"

Cash lit a cigarette. "Yeah."

"Found her yesterday, maybe Friday night. Everyone is talking about hippie drifters or maybe a Charles Manson walking the woods. We usually don't have this many folk in church come Sunday." She gestured at all the parked cars. "People are kinda creeped out."

"Is she dead?"

"Yeah. Folks are gossiping like crazy. Hit over the head, it sounds like. Not shot. We always have at least one person shot during hunting season." She shook her head, looking out across the road. "But folks are saying this just happened. Said her family lives up around Lake George area."

"Any place around here to get a cup of coffee?"

"They got a pot on in the basement of the church."

"Nah, that's all right. I got a sip left in my Thermos. Was just hoping for a hot cup."

"Let me run in and grab you one."

Before Cash could say, *Nah, that's all right,* Debbi walked back to the church as fast as her Sunday high heels would allow. She was back out in a minute, carefully carrying two foam cups. She handed one to Cash along with two sugar cubes. "Didn't know if you wanted cream or not."

"This is good. Thanks." Cash dropped in the sugar cubes, blew at the steam rising from the cup and ventured a small sip. "Anything open around here to get some gas?"

"Not on Sunday. Maybe over in Ada."

They sipped their coffee as they watched cars pull out of the church parking lot and head in various directions. Dad was the driver, the mom in the front passenger seat. Two, three, sometimes four kids scrunched into the back seat. All on their way home to Sunday dinner. And like in any small town, all of them would talk about the Indian girl in the Ranchero and wonder how the waitress from the Red Apple knew her.

"Someone said the woman's name was Edie Birch. The other gossip is that maybe she was going to church out there on the prairie. The church you keep asking about." Pink lipstick stained the edge of Debbi's coffee cup.

Cash wondered how Debbi could possibly be warm standing outside in the cool spring air. Yes, she was wearing a winter coat over her dress, but she was wearing nothing but nylons on her legs. Cash felt cold just looking at her, and she reached over and turned up the heat in the truck. The blast of warm air felt good.

Debbi continued. "What are you doing in town on Sunday anyways?"

Cash shrugged.

"Did you go out to that church?" Debbi shook her head. "Curiosity killed the cat."

"Do you know where that Pastor Steene lives?"

"There's a parsonage out by the church. That's all I know."

"Well, I better head back into Ada and fuel up."

"Have a good drive. Remember, curiosity killed the cat." Debbi started to walk away.

Cash checked her fuel gauge. Not enough to drive back roads. Probably not even enough to get her back to Fargo. "Hey," she called after Debbi, "you know what time it is?" The clock in the Ranchero had long ago died.

Debbi checked a slim silver watch on her wrist. "Almost eleven-thirty."

"Thanks." Cash made a U-turn and headed back to the tar road that would take her across the prairie and back to Ada. The gas station stayed open on Sunday until noon there. She made it into town just as the attendant was cleaning up around the pump area. She hopped out of the Ranchero and leaned against the cab of the truck while he filled the tank for her, took her cash, gave her change and closed up the station. Cash watched the occasional car drive by. She didn't know what to do. The day was still early. All her studies were done. The bars were only serving 3.2 and no one except Ol' Man Willie would be at the Casbah at this hour.

The attendant locked the station door and walked by on the way to his car. "Better put some air in that back tire," he said just before getting in his car. Cash walked to the rear of the Ranchero. Damn, the passenger side was low. She pulled the truck up by the air hose and the attendant came back to help. Gave some extra air to the other tires. Then they both got into their vehicles. He turned left out of the station, and Cash drove south to Moorhead. She decided to go see Al about the tires Hank said he had.

When Cash pulled into Al's driveway, all she could see were his legs poking out from under a jacked-up vehicle. He was lying on a mechanic's creeper. She got out of the Ranchero and stood by the old Ford he was under.

"Just a sec." His voice was muffled under a half-ton of steel.

After a few *thunks* of metal on metal and a couple of swear words, Al pushed himself out. His hands and face were covered with grease.

"Hey. What brings you around?" He looked happy to see her as he wiped his hands on a grease rag. "Tire working out okay?"

"Yeah. But Hank said you had three more?"

"Sure. Sure. Got them back there alongside the garage."

"I think I need 'em. Another tire is leaking air now."

He slapped the Ford with the grease rag. "I'm done with this wreck. Patched the muffler up. Let me get it down and backed out of here, and you can pull yours into the work spot."

He turned back to the car and lowered the jack. Once the spot was free, Cash pulled the Ranchero into the driveway.

"I can put them on this afternoon if you want. But I haven't eaten. Was gonna make myself a grilled cheese sandwich when I got done with that. Mind if I eat first? I'll make you a sandwich."

"I could eat."

"Come on in. Let me get washed up."

Cash sat at the kitchen table and looked around. On her first visit she had watched Al more than take in her surroundings. It was an old house. The cupboards looked like they were made from varnished plywood. The linoleum on the floor was the same old Sears special many of the area farm kitchens had. There was a toaster on the counter and a dishtowel hung over the oven handle. A few dirty dishes sat in the sink. A yellow telephone hung on the wall by the fridge, its long curly cord down the wall, the handset filled with grease stains she assumed to be from Al. A calendar with hunting dogs hung on a nail in another wall. From where she was sitting, she could see into the living room, could see the edge of the couch and corner of the table his television sat on. His house looked lived in. Like a home. In her place, her apartment—if you took away her clothes—you'd never know that someone actually lived there.

"How'd you get this house?" she asked when he came back into the kitchen, grease removed from his hands.

"GI Bill."

He took a frying pan out of the oven, bread and cheese out of the fridge, a beer for him, a beer for her, butter on a plate from inside a cupboard and set about making grilled cheese sandwiches. As Cash watched him, her mind drifted. She liked her apartment, but she knew it was a temporary home. What Al had here was permanent. It had never occurred to her that she might be able to own a home that no one could tell her to leave.

Al broke into her thoughts. "One or two?" he asked.

"One."

He had three sandwiches. She ate her one but was still hungry. She figured it was the best grilled cheese she had ever had, but she didn't say anything. When the sandwiches were gone, he put their dishes in the sink, then finished his beer leaning on the counter, looking at her. She started to feel self-conscious, so she jumped up and put her coat back on, grabbed her beer off the table and walked outside. He came after her and said, "I'll get them tires on for you."

Cash didn't know what was going on with her. She had worked around men since she was eleven. Knew the ins and outs of talking with them, working with them, drinking with them. She had heard some of the raunchiest stories and learned not to let any of it faze her. Roll with the flow was her motto. Something felt different here.

Al worked easily. The tires were already on rims that fit her Ranchero. He explained that some guy's kid kept slipping the clutch on his car during driver's ed. Al had fixed the clutch for him on that car and part of his payment was these four tires off another vehicle the guy had. He jacked up the Ranchero three times, loosened the lug nuts, took the wheel off, put a wheel on. Cash stood around. She smoked cigarette after cigarette once her beer was done. When he wasn't looking, she pulled the cash out of her pocket and counted it. Sixty dollars in bills and a handful of change.

When Al finished the last tire, he put the jack back into his garage, came out wiping his hands on another grease rag. "There you go. Get to Canada and back now if you want."

Cash handed him the roll of bills. "That's all I got for now."

He slowly counted them. Scratched his chin. "Well, here,

whyn't you just give me ten for each?" He handed her back three tens.

"Nah, keep it. I still owe you for the first tire." She refused to take back the money. She got in and pulled the door shut. The window was open, and Al held the door with both hands. They looked at each other for a good bit. Cash broke her gaze first, put in the clutch and brake and turned on the ignition.

"Good seeing you, Cash. Like the hair," he said and moved his hands off the door.

She backed out of the driveway. Once she was out of sight of his house, she hit the steering wheel. *Stupid. Stupid. Stupid. What the hell was wrong with her, acting like an idiot? Damn.* She drove straight west out of Fargo. All the way to Valley City. Straight road. Flat prairie. Home. The drive, the cigarettes, the never-ending-ness of the prairie calmed her. Took her close to an hour to get to Valley City, then she turned around and headed back to Fargo. Powered on the radio. Cracked the window to pull the smoke out the side. By the time she drove past the West Acre Mall, Cash was back to herself.

She went to her apartment. She looked around at the bare walls. Wondered what she might want to decorate it with. A calendar? Fancy curtains? New dishes? She had no idea. She was so used to having nothing of her own, it never crossed her mind before seeing Al's house that she might want something more. Use some of her earnings to get herself something. She had her cue stick. Her .22. A few changes of clothes. And, of course, her Ranchero. Right now, she needed more money from the stash in her dresser to go to the Casbah and a change of clothes. She was sure everyone would laugh her out of the bar if she walked in with her hair in an updo and a fancy cotton blouse on. She yanked the hairpins from her hair and quickly did it in one braid down her back. She put on a T-shirt, tucked a pack of cigarettes in the back pocket of her jeans when the phone in the kitchen rang twice, then quit. She looked at it from across the room. It started to ring again. *Must be Wheaton.*

"Hello."

"Cash? Al here. Wondering if you would want to go shoot some pool. They opened that new pool hall just south of town. Big tables."

Cash pulled the handset away from her ear and looked at it. She heard, "Cash?" She put the receiver back to her ear.

"Yeah?"

"Is that a yeah, you're Cash, or a yeah, you'll come shoot some pool?"

"Both." And she hung up. Stood there.

The phone rang again. She picked it up.

"Al here again. How about if I pick you up around eight?"

Cash panicked. "No! I'll meet you there. I'll meet you there," and hung up again.

She sat with a *thud* at the kitchen table. *Damn.* She dealt out a hand of solitaire. Played the devil. All of a sudden, right there in her own apartment, she got a flash picture of her mom, sitting at their kitchen table, a solitaire game spread out before her. Cash could see a small version of herself standing nearby. That tiny Cash looked up at her mom and asked, "*What you doing, Mom?*" Her mom grinned down and replied, "*Playing the devil.*"

On the dark wood table, in her apartment, grown Cash had all aces up top. She turned over the 2 of clubs and moved all the cards up. *Beat that, devil!* She got up and got a beer from the fridge. Checked the time on the clock on her bedroom dresser. It was already 7:30.

She stood in her bedroom that she knew was supposed to be a living room. The sheet her brother had tacked over the door to give her some privacy when he stayed with her, camped out on her kitchen floor, was draped on a nail pounded into one of the doorframes. She couldn't take the sheet down, that would erase a memory of him, but with it pinned back she had more breathing room at night.

The landlord hadn't fixed the screen Mo had cut when he scaled the brick wall. A torn corner moved slightly in a breeze. Streetlights were on outside. Cash reached over and pulled the thin curtain shut. Her clean laundry was on the stuffed chair at the foot of the bed—the blouse she had removed thrown on top. Her dirty laundry was on the floor. Her bed unmade.

Cash turned around and looked at her kitchen. The toaster from Mo sat on the counter, crumbs all around it. A messy butter stick, still half-wrapped in its own paper, sat next to the toaster. Crumbs all around that too. Mo's deck of cards on the table near a pile of college textbooks. A broom and dustpan leaned against the fridge. She looked back into the bedroom. Other than her clothes and textbooks, there was absolutely nothing about her in the whole apartment. She leaned against the doorframe and took a swig of beer. *Wait,* she laughed to herself. *My beer is in the fridge. My pool money's in the top dresser drawer.*

She pushed herself off the doorframe, put on her winter coat and scarf and headed down to her Ranchero.

It took her a bit to find the new pool hall in south Moorhead. It was in a building that looked like a pole barn. Maybe it was. It had a small sign overhead that read CLYDE'S BILLIARDS. Billiards, a step up from a pool hall or a beer joint, she supposed. She found a spot in the parking lot—about twenty other cars were already parked. She smoked a cigarette and looked around. A young white couple exited their car a row over and walked up to the door, his arm across her shoulder, a cue case in his other hand. When he opened the door, Cash caught a glimpse of the interior. Long fluorescent lights hung over nine-foot tables. Folks bent over the tables or leaned on their cues. And then the door shut.

Cash took a deep breath and got out of the Ranchero. She reached for her cue from behind the seat and walked into Clyde's. It was warm and smoky. Al was shooting pool at a table by himself. Cash needed a beer and a cigarette. She walked up to the cashier and asked for a beer. The guy looked at her and said, "All we got is pop, chickadee." *Well, damn that all to hell.* Just then, Al appeared beside her.

"I already got us a pitcher of Coke."

Cash nodded and headed to the table he had been playing at. She took out her cue, put it together and waited. Al lifted billiard balls out of the table pockets and redid a rack. "Wanna break?"

"Nah, you go ahead." Cash needed time to adjust.

They played 8-ball, last pocket. Neither talked much. *Good shot. Nice. Damn. Missed that one.* Cash's nerves calmed down after about three games, and she got her zone back. The Coke was too sugary for her, so she got a glass of ice water and sipped on that. At some point in the night, Tezhi and Bunk came in. When they waved at Cash, Al asked if they wanted to play doubles. They played partners for a string of games.

Close to 10 P.M., the billiard hall door opened. A tall, young woman with hair longer than Cash's, carrying a beaded cue case, walked in. She was followed by an equally tall guy. When Cash watched her take her cue out, she noticed the handle of the stick was beaded in a geometric design of orange and blues. They were given a spot four tables down from where Cash and Al were playing.

Tezhi said, "There's your competition, Cash."

"Who's that?"

"Shyla GoodPlenty."

"She's Crow," added Bunk.

"Thought she was Cheyenne?"

"Your turn, Al," said Cash.

"Watch her shoot," said Tezhi.

Cash did. Both Shyla and her boyfriend were excellent shots. Cash couldn't tell if Shyla was better than her or not. Cash doubted it. The only person she had ever seen who could truly shoot better than herself was her brother. Once in a while, her tournament partner, Jim. Shyla's boyfriend saw Cash watching. He tipped his pop glass in her direction.

"Come on, Cash. Your shot."

"Where did she come from?" Cash asked Bunk as she bent over the table, her cue stick lined up at a striped ball.

"She goes to school at Concordia. Started spring quarter. If you ever came to the Indian students' meeting, you'd know. Her boyfriend's name is Terry." Bunk lowered her voice. "I think they're Mormons. They don't drink or smoke. I'm surprised they shoot pool."

Cash ran the rest of the stripes before missing a long shot on the 8-ball.

"It's up to you, Al," Cash said, then went back to watching Shyla play.

Cash and Al won the game against Tezhi and Bunk. Before they could re-rack, Shyla's boyfriend walked over and said, "How about we play the winner?" He pointed his cue at Tezhi and Bunk. "You guys can shoot on our table if you want."

"I think I want to watch," said Bunk, hopping on a stool, lighting up a cigarette. Tezhi joined her.

"I'm Terry. This is Shyla."

"Al. Cash. Rack 'em up."

Cash had never played against a woman who shot as good as she did. Most of the women in the bars only shot pool to keep an eye on their husbands or boyfriends. None of them were really serious about the game. Al was proving to be good competition for Cash. Tezhi and Bunk were fun to play. They both tried hard, and neither got mad when they lost. Terry, this new guy, was a good shot. Shyla was clearly as good as Cash. The difference seemed to be that while Cash had learned from Mo that it was possible to cut almost any shot in, Shyla couldn't seem to miss a bank shot.

Tezhi and Bunk left at eleven, saying they had classes first thing in the morning. The other four kept playing, equally matched. At midnight, Shyla said, "I gotta get back to the dorm. I don't want to get locked out." She took one last half-hearted shot at the 8-ball, then broke down her cue.

Terry did the same. "Good game, folks. Let's do this again."

"I should go too. I got school in the morning." Cash picked stripes and solids out of the pockets and put them in the storage tray. They broke down their cues and put them in their cases. Al picked up the tray and went to the cashier. When Cash saw him reach into his back pocket for his wallet, she quickly pulled some bills out and held out a five to him.

"I got this." He refused to look at her or take the money. She felt dumb holding it out and finally stuffed it back into her pocket.

They walked out together.

"My car's over this way," Al said.

"My truck's right there."

"Want to grab a bite to eat?"

"I got school in the morning." Cash kept walking toward the Ranchero, then suddenly stopped, turned around, and asked, "How did you get my number?"

"I looked it up in the phone book."

"The phone book?"

"The phone book. Renee Blackbear. Shorty told Hank your name."

Damn. Cash didn't know her name was in a phone book. "Oh." She turned to walk toward her truck.

"This was fun. I'll call," Al called after her.

Cash turned around again. "How come you hung up and then called back?"

He laughed. "I got nervous." He stood there with both hands inside his pockets, his cue case rested in the crook of his arm.

"I usually don't answer my phone." Pause. "I don't like it."

"Well, I'll still try."

They stood looking at each other, a long stretch of parking lot between them.

"If you let it ring four times, then hang up, then call back. You could try that. I might answer. I mean, if I'm home, I'd answer." Cash made it to her Ranchero and drove out of the parking lot before she could say anything more stupid. When she looked in her rearview mirror, Al was standing there, watching her drive away.

Cash went home that night and unplugged her phone from the wall jack. She didn't know what to think about Al. Jim was easy—all he wanted was a quickie and to go home to his wife. No attachments. No drama. Things seemed different with Al, and it confused her. She wasn't used to people wanting her. People seeing her as a person.

At the beginning of the week, Cash had driven to the police station in Ada and told Wheaton about Edie Birch, who was found dead over on Little Lake. *Maybe Wheaton would want to check in with Hubbard County?* Wheaton said he'd do that. He added that he and Geno were taking the train down to Santa Fe over her spring break to check out the Indian art school. Geno would stay if he liked it. Wheaton said he had tried to call Cash and let her know but only got a busy signal. He asked her to check and make sure her phone was on the hook. He told her he would be back before she knew it and let her know he'd found someone to watch Gunner while they were gone.

Cash had then walked over to Wheaton's house to say hi and bye to Geno, who ended up telling her he thought Wheaton had a girlfriend.

"No, he doesn't."

"I think he does," Geno answered. "He sure has been spending a lot of nights driving over to Twin Valley to eat dinner."

"As long as I've known Wheaton, he's liked the café food in Twin Valley. Folks over there don't hound him like they would if he tried to eat here in Ada. Anyways, I've never seen him with anyone."

"Well, he seems happier, more relaxed every time he comes back from eating over there. I know what it looks like when a guy has a crush on someone." Geno grinned.

"Nah, having that little mutt is what's mellowed him out."

"Nah, he's got a girlfriend," Geno had said.

"I'll believe it when I see it," were Cash's parting words.

She walked back to the jail and found Wheaton sitting behind his desk, Gunner at his feet, steadfastly ignoring Cash. She studied Wheaton until he looked up from the newspaper he was reading—crime was at a low, apparently—and said, "What?"

"Nothing."

"You're staring at me."

"Have a good trip. See you when you get back."

"All right, Cash. Pass your exams. See you when I get back. Make sure your phone is on the hook." He went back to reading the newspaper on the desk in front of him. Cash didn't move. "What?"

"Nothing. Have a good trip."

She turned and left.

CASH WAS BORED OUT OF her mind. She'd spent most of
her life working in the fields and shooting pool. This going
to school thing was not how she had ever envisioned her life.
She went over to Halstad from Wheaton's jail and stopped
at Arnie's bar. Asked around about any jobs, if anyone was
hiring. Nope. She crossed the street to the second bar in town
and inquired there. Folks gave her the same response with
different words. "*Gotta let the fields dry up some. Then we'll
harrow. Plow. Plant. You know how it goes, Cash. Been doing
this long enough—you should know better than to ask this
early after a flood.*"

She drank a couple beers. Shot a couple games in each
bar before she headed back to Fargo-Moorhead for another
boring day of classes, typing, and a night at the Casbah. She
didn't go back to Clyde's Billiards, although she was tempted.
Shooting pool against Shyla had been a good challenge.

During the week, she'd slept with Jim just to get the confu-
sions of Al out of her mind. It worked. She felt more herself,
more settled. More in charge.

The following week, she went to the classes where attendance was mandatory. Typed papers up in the Indian Students'
office and handed them in. Took the midterm exams in all
her classes. The school would close for spring break over the
Easter holiday.

Cash had figured out a system where she could carry
twelve college credits, test out of the easiest ones, then take

only one or two classes that required attendance. The others she would show up just to take the required tests. Judo was the class she showed up for, no matter what. In fact, she had signed up for it a second time, even though she had completed the requirement once. She figured she needed all the help she could get; she was tired of finding herself in tough spots she couldn't fight her way out of.

In schoolyard and barroom fights, she could hold her own. But recently, working with Wheaton, bigger folks than her had gotten the best of her. In the first instance, it had been Geno and his brothers and sisters who had jumped her in the woods and tied her up. She was way outnumbered. But the guys who killed Geno's father had grabbed her in the dark outside a bar in Halstad and held her in a shack out of town. She had managed to surprise attack one of them and get away. The next time someone got the better of her, she had been drugged and then held with a group of young women who were being trafficked. She'd escaped, with the girls, from that situation by climbing out a second-story window and all of them being rescued by her brother. She hoped that once she learned judo, she would be able to hold her own in any situation against any size person.

By Friday, with all her schoolwork completed, she was ready to drive to Mahnomen for another run at the church. She wasn't sure if the church had anything to do with the woman in the basement of the hospital or the woman at Little Lake, but she felt pulled to go there. She also wanted to know something about the little ones buried in the churchyard . . . and the dark shape that didn't want her around.

She grabbed the green pouch Jonesy had given her, threw a change of clothes in a paper bag, just in case, and locked up the apartment. She put the pouch in the glove box. Before she left town, she went to the Standard station and bought a five-gallon gas can that she filled and set in the back of the Ranchero. Hank, holding a grease-stained rag in equally grease-stained hands, informed her Al had tried to call her, but all he got was a busy signal. Al had asked him how the tires were holding up on her truck. Cash pointed at the wheels, got in her Ranchero and drove off.

Cash decided to cruise by the church on her way to Mahnomen. She had figured out which back roads took her in that direction. On the gravel road on the way to the church, she passed a farmstead. A woman, who might have been the pastor's wife, was hanging sheets and clothes on a line in the yard to dry. Cash didn't slow down to make sure. A quarter of a mile down, she passed the church and no dark boogeyman came creeping around the corner to scare her.

She drove directly to the Red Apple. Debbi set a cup of coffee down and asked, "Just missed the breakfast menu. Roast beef sandwich?"

"Sounds good. Do you work every day, Debbi?"

"Only job in town. Unless I want to be the lunch lady over at the school. Will take old farmers over kids any day." She laughed. "Have your food out in a sec."

Debbi came back in a few minutes with the hot roast beef.

She also carried a second cup of coffee and slid into the seat across from Cash. "Got me a short break here before the noon rush. Old man Einer, the ageless farmer, always eats here. Then sometimes the bankers will come in. Big rush." She sipped her coffee. "Are you back prowling churchyards?"

"I guess. I'm curious. Never seen anything like it—the singing, hands raised. Nothing like the prim and proper Lutherans I've been around. How long have they been out here?"

"Oh, I don't know. Guess I first heard about them four, five years ago. Maybe even six years ago. I mean, the church has been there forever. Used to be an old Lutheran church, Scandinavian immigrants, mostly. Then I think it might have been a branch of the ELC that didn't want to join the larger synod when it changed over." Debbi took another sip of her coffee, stretched her legs up and put her feet on Cash's side of the booth. "Then I remember folks talking about it being a spiritualist church. Apparently, some of the old folks, I mean old folks from the old country, were doing some kind of hands-on healing services. Then this Pastor Steene showed up. That's when things started to really shake out there. We heard rumors it became less of laying on of the hands and more just laying." Debbi winked. "Least that's what I've heard." She took another sip.

Cash kept eating. This encouraged Debbi to continue.

"I've seen him and his wife at the Five and Dime. He's really good-looking. I mean, really good-looking. His wife is pretty. But quiet. He's the one who does all the talking. She just kinda follows him around. And every time I saw her, she was looking at baby clothes. I thought they must have a couple kids at least."

Cash swallowed her food. "I didn't see any at church the other weekend."

Debbi shrugged.

"Can you tell me anything more about the woman up at Little Lake?" Cash asked.

"She's from Leech Lake, but her family lives up there by Lake George. Not here like I thought. And, yeah, she was going to that church. Guess a good handful of Indians go. My aunt says the talking in tongues is almost like spirits-talking. One of the things that attracts them to the church. Reminds them of the old ceremonies or something. I don't know anything about it. Just what my aunt says. There is some gossip that says her family isn't going to let that church bury her. She's going to be buried up around where they live."

She slid her feet off the seat next to Cash and got up to grab a newspaper off the counter. She brought it back and opened it to the obituary page. "That's what I thought. Look, they're having the services for her at one o'clock today. There's a small church this side of the village." She slid the paper toward Cash.

"Guess I should make a run to Lake George, huh?"

"I thought you would say that. I can fill your Thermos for you if you got one."

Cash went out to the truck and grabbed hers, brought it

back in for Debbi to fill. She paid Debbi, then headed out of Mahnomen.

By the time she got to the church just outside of the tiny village of Lake George, a line of cars, headlights on, was driving toward her. She pulled off to the side to let them pass, then pulled in behind the last one. She followed the funeral procession a couple miles before it turned off into a grove of pine trees to a small cemetery. A fresh pile of dirt indicated where the coffin would be let down into the earth.

Cash parked and walked up to stand behind the mourners. A black-suited pastor was the only white man at the graveside. He said a few words, a prayer, and the family shoveled the first clods of dirt into the grave. The mourners started to leave soon after. Cash stood to the side to let them pass. They looked at her, but no one talked to her. The pastor walked by Cash, then turned back around. "Were you a friend of the deceased?"

His question surprised Cash. Without thinking, she said, "We went to the same church."

He shook his head. Looked off into the distance. "Worshipping God is the right thing to do. Not every place is the right place to do that." He began to walk away.

"Why?"

He turned back, looked at Cash. "You're young. So was she. You have your whole life ahead of you. One of the commandments is, 'Thou shalt have no other Gods before me.' My church is working hard to turn your people into good, God-fearing people. Get them away from the heathen worship your folks are used to. But that mumbo-jumbo, laying on of hands, is the work of the devil also. Best that a young woman like yourself not get involved in that." He tilted his head toward the grave. "Nothing good will come of it."

"Are you saying she is dead because of the church?"

"Not my place to speak ill of the living or the dead." He turned and left.

After all the cars drove off, Cash went to the grave. A wreath of flowers lay on the dirt. *What can you tell me?* she asked the grave. A bird tweeted. A rabbit hopped across the other side of the graveyard. A sadness rose from the dirt at her feet and traveled up to her chest. The pines sighed in the wind. Their swaying branches sounded like crying. Cash entered that space of out-of-body-ness. In her mind's eye, she saw a human figure carry a body and lay it at the edge of a lake. Just then, a car passed by the graveyard. The crunch of gravel and a small cloud of dust broke Cash's concentration. The rabbit sat staring at her. A robin, the first bird of spring, hopped over and sat on a gravestone. Cash left the graveyard and headed back toward Mahnomen.

When she reached the outskirts of Mahnomen, she decided to keep going to Ada. She pulled into the hospital parking lot and gave herself a pep talk as she smoked a cigarette. She told herself she had nothing to be afraid of, then shook her body to brace herself to go into the hospital basement alone. She had never been down there without Wheaton. The steps echoed louder than she remembered. She pushed open the swinging doors. The room was empty. She had been afraid of running into Doc Felix on her own, but being alone in the room of the dead might be even worse.

There wasn't a body lying on the steel table. No dark shadow stood in the corner. On one wall was a door with a heavy metal handle. It was the door to the cooler of dead bodies. It looked just like the kind of refrigerator farmers had in their barns to store milk or eggs during the week.

Cash walked tentatively over to the door. She looked behind herself to make sure Doc Felix hadn't entered the room, then opened the door and stepped into the cooler, which was big enough for two steel tables with room to walk between them. On one table was an older gentleman. His beard was gray and his hair was white. He was wearing a navy blue suit and tie. On the other table, still covered with just a sheet, was the woman.

Cash turned to her and put her hand on her chest. It was cold. She willed herself into her meditative state—shut out the coldness of the room and her worry about Doc Felix. *Tell me something*, was her thought. The image that came was someone carrying a body and putting it by a small stream. At that moment, Cash heard a screech.

It took her a split second to realize it was the cooler door and not a sound from the meditative state. She whipped around to see Doc Felix grinning at her from the doorway. He pulled the door shut behind him. "Curious, huh? You seem to have a fascination with dead bodies, little girl. Or did you just stop by to visit me, what with Wheaton out of town and all?" He reached out and grabbed her bicep. "You got a thing for older men, do you? How about you give old Doc Felix a kiss?"

He pursed his lips and tried to lean toward her face while pulling her to him. Cash could smell onion and old sausage on his breath. She tried to twist her arm out of his grasp, but the space in the cooler didn't leave room to maneuver. She ducked her head and his lips smeared across her forehead. Rage engulfed her. Acting on age-old lessons learned in schoolyard fights, she kneed him in the groin. Then she elbowed him in the middle of his back as he doubled over. She pushed him off to the side, causing Doc Felix to fall on the old man in the navy-blue suit, propelling the cart into the wall. Cash ran out of the hospital basement.

Back in her Ranchero, she gunned it out of the parking lot. Five blocks away, she pulled over in front of a white two-story house with a picket fence. It took two cigarettes before she stopped shaking.

She slammed her hand on the steering wheel. Cussed every swear word she knew. Lit another cigarette. Looked behind her. He hadn't followed her. Then she started laughing. Her judo training had kicked in. Although kneeing someone in the groin wasn't exactly a judo move, the elbow in the back was. Cash doubted he would say anything to Wheaton. He had enough on his mind without having to think she couldn't take care of herself against the likes of dirty Doc Felix. Still laughing nervously to herself, she headed back toward the church on the prairie.

The clothes on the clothesline were still hanging. Cash

was pretty sure it was the parsonage. She didn't see any kids playing in the yard. At the church, she pulled in alongside a gray sedan parked there.

She didn't see the dark shadow, and after her little bout with Doc Felix, she was feeling a bit surer of herself. She got out of the Ranchero and walked to the church entrance, shoulders back with confidence. The door was unlocked, so she went in. The church felt quiet without the organist thumping out music and the pews full of parishioners. There were bouquets of white lilies on the altar. They filled the air with a thick, sweet scent.

Pastor Steene, wearing a stiffly ironed white dress shirt and dress slacks, stepped out from a side door behind the altar. He was still wearing his shiny, pointed leather shoes. "Welcome. Glad you came back to visit us. What's your name, child?"

"Renee Blackbear." She wasn't about to give him the name she considered to be her real one. "And I'm not a child."

"We are all children in the eyes of God." He moved down the aisle toward her—his movement reminded her of a barn cat slinking toward a mouse in the haymow. She stepped backward.

He stopped. "There is nothing to be afraid of here." He changed his demeanor and came at her in a brisk but relaxed pace. "We can step outside and talk. The lilies are kind of overpowering in this old building." He brushed past Cash and stepped outside. She followed.

She hadn't realized she was holding her breath until they got outside, where she gulped fresh air.

"What brings you back this holy weekend?"

Holy weekend? That's right, it is Easter weekend. "I just stopped to see if you had services tonight. Good Friday, right?"

"Yes. Seven in the evening. Are you from around here?"

"Over by Ada."

His eyes captured hers. Held her gaze. "You've found the right place. We are a small church. But growing. A family in Christ. With prayer, we ease the pain. Suffering goes away. The holy spirit washes away the sins of all." His cadence, his way of speaking, caused Cash to feel like she was going into one of her meditative trances. She jerked her eyes away from him, toward the graveyard, and saw the dark being standing there. As long as the shadow stayed where it was, she decided she was fine. She coughed to clear her throat and settle her nerves.

"I drove by here last fall. Saw the new grave over there."

He looked surprised, then glanced to the graveyard. The dark being hadn't moved, nor did Pastor Steene seem to notice it. "A sad loss for our family. I do believe the Lord is testing our strength as a family. Are you familiar with the story of Job?"

Cash shook her head no and thought, *I'm not interested in knowing either.* Instead, she asked, "Is that your house back there?"

He gazed down the road in the direction she pointed. "Yes." He checked the watch on his wrist. "It's almost dinner time. The wife will have prepared a good meal. You could join us, then come to services tonight." Cash was getting ready to say no, she'd wait here until services, but then she heard a laugh from the dark being in the graveyard.

She nodded yes.

He offered to drive her back to the house and then bring her to services, but Cash had learned her lesson when a college professor down in St. Paul had talked her into riding in his car. Nope, she was not getting in a car with some random dude, no way. Not even a pastor.

At the farmhouse, the man waited for Cash to park behind him. As he opened the door to the house, he called out, "Lillian, we have a guest. She's come back for services tonight. I told her we have enough pot roast for a guest."

Cash watched Pastor Steene's wife. Lillian. She had greeted them at the door and smiled a welcome. Just like at the church, the smile didn't reach her eyes. She stared Cash up and down, the way high school girls graded each other's appearance. Lillian was tall and thin, with her dark hair done up in a French roll. She put out another place setting. There were no children running around and the family portrait on the piano in the living room was just the two of them, dressed for their wedding day.

Cash was on edge. She declined a glass of water, recalling it was a drugged cup of coffee that had gotten her from a cathedral to a pimp house. She was upset with herself for being so wary but, at the same time, two Indian women were already dead and she didn't plan to be a third. Then she discounted her own thinking. These church people might be strange, but they were people of God. She was having trouble telling the difference between her nerves and reality. But the potatoes and beef were delicious. She ate two plates full.

The pastor was charming throughout the meal. He asked Cash about her studies. When he asked about her family, she told him that she had been raised in foster homes. Had a sister she hadn't seen since she was three. She didn't know where her mother was. She didn't know where they lived or even if they were still alive. She told him about her brother, Mo. How he had shown up at her door in the middle of the night after he had finished one tour in Vietnam. That he said he couldn't stand it out here in the real world. How he had stayed with her for about a month before he re-upped for another tour.

She shared things about her life she hadn't shared with anyone other than Wheaton. Some of the abuse in the foster homes. The ones Cash could bring herself to talk about. Both the pastor and Lillian listened attentively. At some point, Lillian warmed up to her. She nodded in sympathy at some of Cash's stories, plied her with good food and kind attention. In Cash's eye, the pastor looked less and less like a cat ready to pounce. Instead, he seemed to radiate real concern and care.

When the pastor said, "It sounds like the people you lived with weren't real Christians," Cash agreed. Some of her misgivings about the couple, about their church and the dark shadow, were chiseled away by the couple's kindness. She even forgot to ask about the two small graves by the church.

She felt soft and small. No one had paid her this much

attention, ever. Wheaton was always there for her, but he was steady, like a rock. Constant. Sure. Solid. Sitting at the pastor's table, Cash felt a warmth and glow in the kitchen that had not been there earlier.

After eating, she stood up and said, "I'll wash dishes, Lillian."

Lillian thanked her and said she had to go change for services, but she would be right back. Pastor Steene remained at the table.

Cash felt his eyes on her as she did the dishes. When Lillian came back, in a go-to-church dress and heels, the dishes were all washed and dried and stacked on the kitchen counter. Cash put on her jacket and went out to the Ranchero. The cold night air was a sudden contrast to the warmth of the kitchen.

Cash declined their offer to ride with them to the church and took her own vehicle. The service was the same as the Sunday before. Lots of pumped-up music and swaying. Lots of hands-on blessings. Cash wasn't in a hurry to leave like the first time, even though she figured once you'd been blessed by God, why go back for more? If once wasn't enough, why bother was her way of thinking. But her perception of the pastor and his care for his congregants had shifted some. She didn't feel as leery as before, and the dark shadow had not appeared again that night.

As before, there were a handful of Indian women in the church. They were all younger, wearing dresses, nylons and pumps. A righteous-looking group. They looked like the kind of women who maybe had a hard life and were now trying to turn their lives around. Cash could imagine them in jeans and T-shirts, shooting pool at the Casbah.

After services, everyone filed out, shook hands with the pastor, even Cash, and stood around the church lot. Huddled in small groups against the cold spring air, the men smoked off to the side of the building, while the women pretended they didn't smoke. Cash joined the small group of Indian women.

"Hey."

The women nodded hello. They continued talking softly about the service, commenting on how grateful they were to find a place that accepted them for who they were. One of them commented in an even lower voice, "Doesn't hurt to have a good-looking pastor." None of the women in congregation hid their admiration of the man. The others laughed behind their hands. "Just be careful his wife doesn't catch you looking at him." They all laughed some more.

Cash wondered what they meant. Lillian had warmed to her. She also thought, *If you didn't all crush on him, maybe his wife would be a bit more friendly to you.* But Cash didn't say anything out loud to them, because what she wanted to do was bring up the woman from Lake George or the woman laying on a metal bed in Ada. So, she just stood and listened to the chatter, aching for a cigarette as the men's smoke drifted her way. She almost missed the comment because her attention was on the tempting smell of cigarette smoke and also furtively looking at the cemetery grounds for the dark shadow.

"Did you go to Edie's funeral?" one of the women said softly.

All the women shook their heads no. Lowered their heads in sorrow or respect.

Cash asked, "Edie who?"

One of the women explained that Edie Birch had come to church for quite a few months, then had disappeared. She was found over in Little Lake just this past week. Someone had dumped her body. Killed her. And she had been pregnant. Her baby was in the hospital over in Detroit Lakes. There was some issue between the tribe and the county 'cause the baby's grandmother wanted to take the baby home, but the nosy old social workers were messing with the family.

The women gossiped some more. They threw out ideas about what had happened. What might happen. *Did anyone know who the father was? Why did the county always have to mess in their business?*

Finally, Cash broke into the conversation. "How did you all find this church?"

They looked at each other, then the woman who had giggled about the pastor's wife said, "Most of us have been going to GED classes in DL. Pastor Steene came to the school the last time I was at class and invited me to services."

There was a chorus of, "That's how I got here too."

"And you like it?"

Another chorus of yeses. "Saved my soul." "Haven't touched a drink in months." "He is so good-looking." "Jesus, save my soul." One of the women made a swooning motion with her hand over her heart. The rest of the group giggled.

"Why are you here, city girl?" one of them asked Cash. "Where are you from?"

Cash shrugged. "Just searching. Like everyone else, I guess."

"Where you from?" was asked again.

"My family was from here, but we were all raised in foster homes."

Another round of gossip ensued about Edie's baby and the evils of the foster care system always messing with Indian families. "Our kids are our kids. I don't know why they can't just leave us alone," one of them said.

"Do you know who you're related to?" someone asked Cash.

Cash shook her head no. This wasn't a conversation she had been prepared to have. Her chest tightened. Damn, she wanted a cigarette. She felt in her pocket. The pack was still there and so were the matches. The men were still smoking.

"You could go to the tribal office and find out. They got a list of everybody over there. Years and years back."

"Sometimes family ain't all it's cracked up to be. I had to move to DL to get away from my crazy family. I got a little girl. Didn't want her raised around all the drinking and crazy uncles, if you know what I mean," another woman interjected.

"Most of us dropped out of school and are now trying to get our lives back on track. Edie was too, rest her soul. And

Lori. Anyone seen Lori lately?" A lot of no headshaking. "Maybe she went back home."

"Who is Lori?" asked Cash.

"Lori? I think she was from Devils Lake. Came over here when she snagged one of the Nodin brothers at United Tribes PowWow in Bismarck. No one around here will date him." All the women in the circle shook their heads in agreement. "Guy's violent as can be. Always jacking his women around. Maybe she just went back home to get away from him and that's why we ain't seen her."

"So, you're from here?" one of the women asked Cash again.

"Yes. No. Family's from here. I live in Fargo." Cash didn't want to go any further in the conversation. "Is there some church law that says we can't smoke?" Without waiting for an answer, Cash lit up. The other women shifted from foot to foot. They glanced nervously at the church doorway. Halfway through her cigarette, the other women decided it was time to go. They drifted off in pairs, each saying their ride was leaving. Cash watched a couple of them light up as soon as the car doors closed behind them. She was left standing alone in the churchyard with the rest of her cigarette.

The pastor and his wife were nowhere to be seen when Cash got into the Ranchero and left the church parking lot. She had hoped to say goodnight to them and thank them again for the dinner, but she also didn't want to go looking for them. She glanced back toward their house on the prairie. The lights inside were on. *All in all*, she thought to herself, *it was a good night.* Good food. Good talk over supper. Maybe the pastor and his wife weren't as awful as she first judged them to be. And that damn dark shadow had kept to itself all night. She also had a possible first name and a home location for the woman in the hospital basement. Although still no idea of how or why she had died, or how she ended up in the floodwaters by Ada.

Cash didn't like the bars in Mahnomen. Every night seemed to end in a drunken fight, so she drove the forty-five minutes back to the Casbah. Just as she was ready to pull into a parking spot, she decided to head over to Clyde's Billiards in Moorhead. She drove through the parking lot and made sure Al's vehicle wasn't there, then she parked, grabbed her cue and went in.

Shyla and her boyfriend were shooting pool. Cash joined them for a game of three-man 9-ball and played until midnight, when Shyla needed to get back to the dorm. Cash then drove back to the Casbah, had a beer, shot two games of pool and called it a night.

CASH SMOKED A CIGARETTE AS she lay in bed. The ashtray was on her chest. The smoke rose to the ceiling. She didn't know what to think. She ran the last week through her mind. The body in the cooler. Doc Felix. Al. Jim. Maybe she needed a John in her life? That thought made her cough on cigarette smoke and spew ashes from the ashtray across the blanket. She quickly brushed them off in case there was an ember in them. When she was sure she hadn't started the bed on fire, she returned to smoking and her thoughts.

Two dead women pulling at her attention. Lori from Devils Lake might be lying in the county hospital, given the conversation with the women at the church. If so, she had either been killed or beaten and left for dead, essentially killing her. Edie Birch clearly had met a different fate. Cash drifted through her memories of being at the gravesite over by Lake George. The person carrying Edie to the river's edge at Little Lake had been obscure enough that Cash couldn't tell if it was a man or woman. Was she already dead? Or was she put into the river still alive and then died? And then there were the two small graves.

Debbi, at the Red Apple, thought the pastor and his wife had some children. When Cash had dinner with them, she didn't see any signs of children living in the house. Nor did they bring any children to the services with them. Where were the babies, if there were any?

Cash shuddered when she thought of the graves in the graveyard. Maybe if they lost their children, they didn't feel comfortable sharing their grief with others. Just like there were things Cash didn't feel comfortable sharing, talking about, with anyone else. She snuffed out the cigarette in the ashtray, reached up and shut off the light, pulled the covers up under her chin and fell asleep.

She dreamt of women swimming through ice-cold floodwaters, and men dressed in black digging holes in black dirt. She woke when sunlight streamed through the thin curtains over the bedroom window. She crawled out from under the covers and threw on some clothes.

She still had days off from school. Wheaton and Geno were on their way to Santa Fe. Bunk and Tezhi had gone back home to White Earth, Bunk's home reservation, for the break. She didn't know where Sharon and Chaské, Sharon's Lakota boyfriend, had gone to. Some hippie gathering far off in the woods smoking pot and drinking Spanada wine, she supposed.

Cash made coffee and a piece of toast. She stood at the kitchen counter, drinking her coffee and chewing her toast while she tried to figure out what to do next. With days off from school, what she really wanted to do was head to the Casbah and drink a few beers. Okay, more than a few, and shoot pool nonstop. She looked at the clock on her dresser. It was only 7:30 A.M. There was no way Shorty would serve her at this hour. What she did instead was grab a couple longnecks from her fridge before heading down to her truck.

She took a slow ride north of town. Driving a steady 50 mph, she watched the muddy fields go by, noting which ones still had floodwater standing between the furrowed rows of dirt and which fields would be dry enough to plow and plant in the coming few weeks—provided the farmer's prayers for no rain were answered. Just south of Perley, she noted a four-door Ford sitting in the ditch on the wrong side of the road. A family car. Its four tires buried in mud and muck. No crash damage. She reckoned some kid on a hot date had tried to show off and made a judgment error in passing another car on the two-lane.

She kept driving through Hendrum and Halstad. Just north of Halstad she turned toward the river. The gravel road had deep ruts and a couple times she was afraid she was going to get stuck in the mud that seeped up through the gravel, but she kept going until she reached the turnoff to the county dump. She parked the truck on the least muddy part of the road and got out. Took the .22 out from behind the seat and proceeded to have target practice at various bottles, tin cans, and piles of garbage sitting around.

Between shots, she could hear the Red River coursing its way up to Canada. The whooshing sound was a different sound than lake water lapping at the shores. The river water was on the move, carrying the floodwaters north. The banks were lined with tall cottonwoods and gnarly oaks that were bare of leaves. The sky was springtime gray. It was still too cold for the sky to be summertime blue. Two red-breasted robins walked around in a nearby field and pecked at the ground for worms or leftover seeds from last fall. Looking around, you would never know that just a week and a half ago the whole Valley had been a lake. Now it just looked like farm country after a heavy spring rain.

When Cash ran out of bullets, she put the .22 back behind the seat and decided to risk driving into the driveway a few feet just to get the Ranchero turned around. Mistake. She spent a good twenty minutes rocking the truck from reverse to first gear, back to reverse and then to first to get it out of the mud. With one final burst of gas and the truck in reverse, the back end fishtailed out of the mud and almost off the other side of the road as she gunned the engine. Once she had the truck back in the center ruts of the road, she headed toward the small town of Halstad.

She stopped at Arnie's bar, dug thirty cents out of her jeans pocket and got a pack of cigarettes from the machine that sat in the doorway to the bar. She waved at the bartender before she headed back out and climbed into her truck again. She debated on whether to drive over to Ada, maybe make another swing through Twin Valley and Mahnomen, but her curiosity wasn't in it today. Two dead women, two dead children. Plus, a black shadow lurking around a graveyard. Her mind needed a break. She lit up a cigarette, searched under the seat for the church key, looked around to make sure no one was watching her when she used the opener to pop the top off the beer that sat between her legs. She started a slow drive back toward Fargo-Moorhead.

The fields were no dryer on the way back than they were going. There was mud all over the road outside of Perley where the Ford car had been pulled out of the ditch. By the time Cash got back to Moorhead, it was almost noon. She figured Shorty wouldn't give her too hard a time if she stopped at the Casbah.

She got her cue stick, threw her stocking cap on the seat and quickly brushed her hair down with cold hands before entering the bar. Shorty saw her come in and put a Coke on the bar. Cash shook her head no. Shorty pushed the bottle of pop in her direction. Cash shook her head no again but took the bottle, and went and put some coins in the metal slots of the pool table without speaking. Two farmers were sitting in a booth drinking 3.2 beer from bottles. Ol' Man Willie was sitting sullenly at the bar. Cash practiced her bank shots. Her cut-in shots. She was in the zone. Nothing fazed her. It was her world. The only thing that could have been better would have been to have a Bud sitting on the bar rail behind her.

She played against herself all afternoon. Every once in a while, one of the farmers would put some coins in the jukebox, and country music would fill the space. The twang of country music, the thud of billiard balls dropping into pockets, the low murmur of men talking about the flood, rain, soybeans, beets and broken farm machinery settled Cash's nerves about murder and jiibay in a way nothing else could. She was home.

On her third trip back from the bathroom, she saw Al standing by the pool table, holding a cue, looking in her direction. He was wearing a shirt that appeared to have been ironed. She was aware of her own wrinkled shirt and the mud on her shoes from standing out in the dump yard. Because she didn't know what else to do, she gave him a slight nod and asked, "Last pocket?"

"Sure."

They played two games, both of which Cash lost. Al made her nervous. *Why was he here?* was the question that kept running through her mind.

"Have you eaten yet?" he asked, sinking the 11-ball in

a side pocket and sending the cue down the rail to put the 12-ball in—the cue stopping just a fraction of an inch without dropping into the pocket.

Cash shook her head no.

"Why don't we go to Shari's Kitchen and grab a bite? I'll pay. And then there's an 8-ball tournament tonight over at the pool hall in Moorhead. Partners?" He finished his run of stripes and missed on sinking the 8-ball, which Cash was pretty sure he flubbed on purpose to prolong the game. "Twelve team bracket. Double elimination. I think we could win."

Cash bent over the table to take aim at the 3-ball. She nicked the 3 instead of hitting it straight on, dropping the cue into the pocket. *Damn*, she thought. She gave a short laugh. "Might be a little off on my game today."

"Nah. You'll be okay. Come on. Let's go eat. I'm buying—food and pool." He stood, holding the bar cue, grinning at her.

"I have to change clothes," Cash said.

"Okay."

"Okay."

"Okay."

Cash shook her head. Broke down her cue, put it in the case and walked out of the bar to her Ranchero. Al grabbed the door just as she was getting ready to get into the truck.

"I can follow you to your place."

"That's okay. I'll meet you at Shari's."

"All right. I'll head there now."

"Okay." Cash pulled the door shut and backed out of the parking spot. She drove the block down to her apartment. When she got out to go upstairs, she looked back at the Casbah and noticed Al was still standing on the street looking after her. He waved, got in his pickup and drove off.

Cash ran upstairs and quickly changed clothes. A clean T-shirt. Clean jeans. And her cowboy boots she had found when cleaning migrant shacks after beet season a few springs back. She brushed and braided her hair in one long braid down her back. One braid was easier to control when leaning over a pool table. Her hair was long enough that she could stick the end of the braid in her back pocket if she needed to keep it out of the way.

Once she had done all that, she stopped in her kitchen, stood without moving. She hadn't let herself think about what she was doing. *It's just a pool game. And you gotta eat.* With that thought, she went down to her truck and drove to Shari's.

Al was already seated at a table that had a red and white checkered tablecloth on it, a cup of coffee on the table between his hands. He grinned when he saw her looking around at the entrance and waved her over.

"Want some coffee?" he asked.

"Nah. Gets me jittery. Maybe just some water."

He pushed a menu across the table to her. "I'm going to get the French dip sandwich."

Cash looked through the menu without reading it. "I'll get that too." She closed the menu and pushed it back toward him.

When the waitress came, Al placed their order. They sipped their drinks without talking.

The waitress came back carrying two plates with French dip sandwiches and set them down in front of them. "Get you anything else right now, doll?" she asked Al.

"Looks good," Al answered. The waitress turned and left. To Cash, he said, "I'm starving. Worked all day rebuilding a carburetor. Guy needs his pickup running before spring field work. You shoot pool all day?"

"Half a day," Cash answered around a mouthful of sandwich.

"Your phone get shut off?"

That question made Cash stop chewing and look at Al.

"I've tried calling, and all I get is a busy signal."

"Might be unplugged."

They went back to eating in silence. When they were both finished, Al got up to pay for the meal at the cash register. Cash wiped her mouth on a paper napkin and went and stood by him while the cashier gave him his change.

"Wanna ride with me?" he asked as he held the door open for her to exit the restaurant.

"I'll drive. Meet you there." Cash hurried to her Ranchero. She pounded her fists on the steering wheel before lighting up a cigarette. She watched Al drive his pickup out of the parking lot and turn down the road in the direction of the new billiard hall. She reached under the front seat and pulled out the long neck she knew was stashed under there. She opened it with the church key. No one was entering or exiting the restaurant, so she guzzled half the beer before turning the truck on and heading in the same direction as Al. She drove slowly and took quick drinks to finish off the bottle. Once finished, she stashed the empty bottle under the seat, pushing it back far enough so it wouldn't accidentally roll forward. She could see Al smoking, waiting for her by the door.

The air in the pool hall was hazy with cigarette smoke and every table had people holding cue sticks—either standing by a table or bent over shooting at a stripe or solid. None of the players were familiar to Cash. It wasn't the bar crowd she was used to. These folks were dressed almost in going-to-church clothes—pressed slacks and button-down shirts. The girls' hair had been ratted up and hair-sprayed into place. Cash felt out of place until she saw Shyla and Terry at the far end of the hall. Shyla saw her and raised her cue stick in greeting. Cash nodded back. She followed Al and watched him pay the entry fee. "There's no more open tables," he said. "Let's go ask Terry if we can run a couple practice games with them."

They played until staff, wearing shirts with crossed cue sticks over front pockets, announced the starting of the tournament. Cash and Al moved up in the brackets on the winning side. Terry miscued on the 8-ball, and he and Shyla got moved to the loser's bracket, where they held their own. Close to the end of the evening, it was clear it was the two Indian teams would play each other for the cash prize.

It was an easy win for Cash and Al. He won the break, neatly sinking the 8-ball right after clearing the table of all solids. There was a lot of handshaking with the other teams that Cash avoided by hugging the wall and holding her cue stick in front of her. Al picked up their winnings and gave Cash her half. She did shake hands with Shyla and Terry and agreed to go for cup of coffee with them and Al at Shari's to celebrate.

Cash drank coffee and picked at a piece of pecan pie while she listened to the other three recap the games of the night—the shots missed, the incredible near misses, and which shooters needed to be watched next time. They were all high from their wins. Shyla and Terry were happy with the money from second place. They swore to get Cash and Al next time.

Cash's body was very aware of Al's thigh resting next to hers in the booth. To distract herself, she let her mind drift to jiibay and dead women until Shyla spoke directly to her.

"You know, we should team up for the women's 8-ball pool tournament. No one can beat us. None of these women know how to shoot."

"Huh?"

"There's a women's 8-ball tournament coming up. You and me together. We could win."

Both of the men jumped into the conversation with "yeah," and "you could, easy." Al said, "I could front the entry fee." When he saw Cash's face shut down, he quickly amended, "My shop could front the entry fee. My business. You could get shirts made with 'Al's Auto Repair' over the pocket, like the losing teams had on tonight."

Everyone laughed.

Shyla leaned forward. "We could make ourselves ribbon

shirts. With ribbons hanging down the back so they won't get in the way when we lean over the table. Come on, Cash. We could win. You and me together. Can't no one beat us."

Cash replied, "I don't know how to sew."

Everyone except Cash laughed good-naturedly. Cash, unsure if they were laughing at her or with her, pulled her leg away from Al's. He put his arm across her shoulders and grinned down at her.

Shyla said, "I know how to sew. Come on. Easy money."

"When is it?"

"Next month, I think. I'll look the next time I go shoot."

"Tomorrow," said Terry.

They all laughed again.

"Okay," said Cash. A good pool game with easy money was hard to turn down. "How much is the entry fee?"

"I'll check," said Shyla.

"I'll pay. My auto shop will pay," Al said once again, as Cash moved her body away from his. "The shop can be your sponsor. That's how you get my name on the shirt pocket."

"Yeah," both Shyla and Terry said.

"I gotta go," Cash said, nudging Al to let her out of the booth.

Al put some money on the table and pushed it toward Terry. "Cover ours?"

Al followed Cash out to her Ranchero. He stood on the pavement, holding the door open, while she was putting the key in the ignition. She couldn't close it without pushing him out of the way.

"Why'nt you come over for a couple beers? We could celebrate our win."

Cash hesitated. Didn't look at him. She pushed in the clutch and brake and turned on the ignition. "Okay."

"Follow me. Or you remember where I live?"

"I remember," she said, reaching out to grab the door handle. He shut it for her.

Cash watched him walk away. She pounded the steering wheel. *Damn. Damn. Damn.* Al, pool, food and beer.

IT WAS AN EASY NIGHT of good beer and good sex on the couch again with cigarettes smoked and light talk about the games they'd won. After a couple hours, Cash went to the bathroom, got dressed and walked to the front door while Al still lay on the couch half-naked, smoke drifting up from his cigarette.

"Hey, Cash," he called right when her hand was on the doorknob.

"Huh?" she asked without really turning around.

"Turn your phone on, would you?"

"I don't like talking on the phone."

"I won't talk. I'll just say, 'Come shoot pool,' and hang up."

That made Cash laugh a tiny bit. She left and pulled the door shut quietly behind her.

The next morning Cash got up, took a bath, got dressed, drank a cup of coffee, filled her Thermos and lost a quick game of solitaire with the devil before heading out. Once in her truck, she headed east to the White Earth Reservation.

Cash didn't have a plan in her mind. She stopped at the Red Apple and chatted with Debbi between customers and eating her own pancakes and eggs. Breakfast finished, she went out to the small graveyard by the weather-beaten church on the prairie. No cars were in the parking lot. With the Ranchero in neutral and the heat turned on, Cash rolled down the window and lit a cigarette. She opened the glove box and retrieved the green pouch Jonesy had given her. She held it tightly in her hand, wishing Geno were in the truck with her.

A few clouds drifted in the sky. Every time one passed in front of the sun, the temperature dropped a couple degrees. Cash watched the graveyard. Nothing moved, except the loose hairs on the top of Cash's head with the light breeze. The dried grass stood still. Another cloud moved on, freeing the sunlight. And then a chill filled the cab of the Ranchero, causing the hair on her arms to stand straight. The black figure emerged from behind the largest pine tree in the graveyard. It stood looking in her direction, although she couldn't tell whether it had actual eyes or not. Her hand tightened on the steering wheel. Her heartbeat quickened. The figure stepped to the side and began walking the perimeter of the graveyard. The message was clear to Cash. *This is mine. Keep out.* For some reason, that arrogance pissed her off. She snuffed out her cigarette, dropped the tobacco pouch on the car seat, shut off the truck and jerked open the car door. As she stepped out, her tennis shoes sunk into the still waterlogged gravel and dirt of the driveway. Cash didn't care; she just stared at the dark figure.

It stopped in front of the two small graves. The figure was like a storm cloud you couldn't see through. Cash took one step toward the graveyard. The darkness grew in size, became taller, thicker. Cash took another step forward. It grew to the size of the small pine tree to its left. Her heart beat loudly in her chest. The air was winter cold and smelled of decay. She looked at the sun; it was no longer emanating heat.

She took another step forward. The darkness leaned its thick self toward her without taking another step. It had no distinct shape, but it gave off the closest feeling to pure evil Cash had ever encountered.

A car door slammed behind her and made her jump. She whipped around to see Pastor Steene walking toward her, a smile on his face. "Renee, what brings you back to our humble place of worship? Lillian went to get the mail and saw your truck in the driveway. We have a good view of the churchyard from the parsonage down the road."

Cash backed away, once again skittish. The presence of the dark shadow had brought back the feelings of not trusting the man. Not wanting him, or anyone, to get close enough to touch her.

"Child, are you afraid? This is a church. I'm a man of God. You're always safe here."

Cash continued to back away. She could feel the wet, soft ground giving way under her shoes. She looked over her shoulder. The dark figure had diminished in size and was now mostly hidden behind the branches of a pine tree. Pastor Steene stood where he was. He looked over at the graveyard.

Cash pointed behind her. "What the heck is that dark shadow that creeps around the graveyard?"

"Dark shadow?"

"You don't see him?"

"No, Renee, I don't. Come here, child. Tell me what you see?"

"A big dark shadow. In this graveyard." Cash took a step forward. "I see it almost every time I come here. Lurking around like some evil demon."

"No one really sees the devil. The devil wears many disguises. The devil on earth can look just like you or me."

"My cousin saw it too," said Cash. "He calls it a jiibay. A ghost of the dead."

The pastor held out his hand. Reached for her. She moved closer and let him take her hand with his, which were warm, almost hot. The rest of her body felt the chill of the spring air more intensely. "Let's go into the church and pray," he said and led her inside. "Sometimes our fears give life to our imagination. It is only the wonder of God that lives around this holy place."

"I see it." Cash was adamant. "I see it with my own two eyes."

Ignoring her claim, the pastor guided her to the front of the church. Told her to kneel beside him in front of the cross. After all the abuse at the hands of the Christian foster families, Cash had no use for prayer. It had never brought any help. She had grown to dislike everything their beliefs held dear. But the pastor's calm voice overrode her distaste, so she knelt with him. Wary, she kept her eyes open as he prayed for her, for her sins, for the salvation of the souls who had harmed her while using God's name in vain. His voice was hypnotic. She felt herself entering the meditative trance she used to enter while sitting on a hard wooden chair for hours as punishment. His voice soothed her fears, calmed her heart rate. Light streamed in the stained-glass windows, casting multicolored sunshine on the cross in front of them.

Cash's body relaxed. The pastor put his hand on her head in the same manner he had laid healing hands on the women during the church service. Hot electricity shot through her body. With his hand still on her head, he continued to pray for her soul, for the evilness to depart. Cash was so caught up in the sing-song rhythm of his words, the soothing cadence, that she didn't notice his hand had moved down her spine. It wasn't until he reached the small of her back that she felt the first stirrings of sexual tension in her lower body.

Cash jerked away. Ashamed that her body had reacted to his prayer and attention in such a manner. She stood, backed away from him. "Uh, I should go."

He stood. Cash looked down at the worn carpet in front of her. She could see where many knees had knelt. She was starting to get cold again, so she pulled her jacket tightly across her chest. "I should go," she said again, her head starting to clear from the daze the pastor's prayer voice had put her in.

She turned and walked down the aisle to the church doorway. She was self-conscious of the pastor following her. *Why did I come here? Why did I come here?* she asked herself over and over. When she stepped outside the church, she stopped on the top step. The dark shadow was back by the two small graves. Pastor Steene stood beside her.

Cash gestured toward the graveyard. "What happened to the children?"

Immediately, the pastor's face saddened. "One never knows when we will be called back home."

He walked past her down the church steps and headed for the graveyard. Cash followed out of arm's reach. She stood opposite from him when they reached the plot. The shadow had faded to nothingness as they approached.

"Our babies. God called them home before their time." His head was bowed, his voice somber.

"Both of them?"

"Who are we to question God's way?"

"I don't think I'd believe in a God that took my kids."

"But you keep returning. There must be something here you are looking for." The pastor looked deeply into Cash's eyes. She felt herself starting to drift out of her body.

"No." *Stay here, stay here.* She wrapped her arms around herself.

"Why are you here, my child?"

"I'm not a child."

"We are all children of God."

Determined not to be distracted, Cash squeezed her biceps

tightly to keep herself grounded in her body and asked, "How did they die?"

"We don't know. God called them in their sleep."

"Both of them? That's not possible."

"Again, who are we to question God's ways?"

Cash was mesmerized by his voice. He spoke in a soft monotone. *What the hell? Is that why I feel drifty? Is he trying to hypnotize me?* She turned away abruptly and looked around the graveyard for the figure. It was nowhere to be seen. The darkest thing in sight was the pastor, all dressed in black.

"I have to go." Cash started to walk away.

"Why don't you come to the house and eat? Lillian was just getting ready to prepare lunch when she saw you over here. Should be ready by now." His voice no longer monotone—he now spoke with normal inflection, with the softness and caring he had used when Cash sat at their table and shared a meal with them before. "Egg salad sandwiches. Nothing special."

Cash was back by the Ranchero. It seemed silly, but the air was warmer there; it felt safer. Less cold. Less thick.

Pastor Steene followed her and stood by his car, the door open. "Come on. Have a bite to eat."

Cash sat in her truck for a cigarette after the pastor pulled out of the church parking lot. She looked toward the graves. No dark figure. She picked up the green tobacco pouch, held it in her hand. She felt the tobacco within the cotton mate- al. She wasn't sure why it calmed her nerves. In her mind's eye, she saw Jonesy putting wood into her woodstove. Jonesy stood up and looked directly at her. Cash opened the glove box and put the pouch safely back inside. She backed out of the church driveway and turned down the road in the direction of the parsonage. All the while talking to herself.

Get a grip, girl. After everything you've lived through, ain't no jiibay in a graveyard gonna scare you. And some old pastor who just wants to pray for your poor heathen soul can't hurt you any worse than anyone else already has. Wheaton wants to know who killed the woman in the morgue. That's your job. Get to it. And you need to eat to keep going. And Lillian sure can cook.

Lunch was just what the pastor promised—an egg salad sandwich on homemade bread. Lillian was wearing a periwinkle blue housedress with a worn apron tied around her waist. She looked young and beautiful and vulnerable. After a short prayer, blessing the food and giving thanks for the retreated floodwaters, they all took a bite of their sandwiches.

Once again, the couple asked Cash questions about her life—her studies at school. A cloud crossed Lillian's face when Cash told them about winning at the pool tournament. "We don't drink," Lillian said. "The devil lives in alcohol."

"We weren't shooting pool in a bar," said Cash. "It's a new place in Moorhead that has pool tables and only serves soda. No one was drinking."

"Billiard halls aren't the most ladylike places for a young woman to hang out in," said the pastor.

Cash almost laughed out loud. She quickly looked dow

at the half-eaten egg salad sandwich on her plate. He had called her a lady, a young woman. *If he only knew.* And, dang, if pool led to hell, she was more than halfway there. Cash quickly changed the subject. "Do you know how to sew?" she asked Lillian. "Your dress is beautiful."

Lillian was pleased with the question. She gave a detailed description of a quilt she was sewing, as well as the piles of fabric she had bought the last time she had gone to the fabric store in Ada. Cash admitted she hadn't sewn anything since a required dress in high school Home Economics. She told a small story about her friend at school who knew how to sew and had offered to make her a new shirt.

When the meal was over, the pastor said his goodbyes. He mentioned he had to make some phone calls from his study and work on a sermon. He took Cash's hand. His other hand held her upper arm lightly in a familiar way. "Come back soon," he said and retreated to a room down the hall.

Cash helped Lillian clean up the lunch plates. Then Lillian insisted on showing off her sewing room. She talked non-stop about her various sewing projects, none of which were baby clothes or blankets, which seemed a bit odd to Cash since the pastor had seemed to imply they had lost infants, who were now in the church graveyard. Although sewing held no real interest to Cash, she decided that with all the attention the pastor got from everyone, Lillian was probably lonely and more than happy to have someone to talk to.

Lillian stood in the doorway as Cash left the house. Cash was surprised when she said, "I like you." Cash didn't know how to respond, so she thanked Lillian for the meal, then waved goodbye when she reached the Ranchero.

Cash drove around aimlessly after leaving the parsonage. She smoked and looked at the waterlogged fields. There was a woman in the county hospital in Ada. Wheaton wanted to know who killed her, but he was off to Santa Fe. Also, if Geno was right, Wheaton maybe had a girlfriend. There was the other woman who was found over here in Mahnomen County. And there were the two babies buried in the graveyard. Goddamn.

She thought briefly about the pastor's hand on the small of her back, but then dismissed the thought. She told herself she was overreacting. The tension created by the dark shadow appearing and disappearing. The tension she had about the graves. She justified it all as being related to attending church. It was bringing up old memories and hurts from people who had called themselves Christians.

She thought about the other kids at school. They were back home with their families, eating chocolate rabbit ears or getting drunk with their friends. She was driving by fields on the open prairie. She hoped they dried up soon so she could get a job plowing or seeding for one of the local farmers. This being Wheaton's right-hand man, when he wasn't even around, wasn't what it was cracked up to be. With her mind finally calmed from the drive, she headed toward Detroit Lakes. Maybe she could find this GED center the women at the church went to. It might be a starting point for finding out more about the two women who had died.

Cash had never spent time in Detroit Lakes, or DL as folks called it. It was a lakeside beach town in the summer. This time of the year, the city population was around five thousand people. Come summer, when Valley farmers and city folks from Fargo-Moorhead migrated to their summer cabins around the lake, the population could swell on any given day to over ten thousand.

On this spring day, a few cars sat in the parking lot of the train depot. The Great Northern ran from the western coast down to the Twin Cities and on to the East Coast from what Cash had heard. A few more cars were parked on Main Street. Cash drove the quiet streets of the town as she looked for a bar where she could stop and maybe get a beer and buy a pack of cigarettes without anyone paying her too much attention. She had heard from Bunk and Tezhi that folks in DL weren't all that friendly to Indians.

On Highway 10, going east, she spotted a bowling alley with a Schmidt beer sign. They would have cigarettes and beer. Apparently, the pastor hadn't managed to wash her of all her sins. She pulled into the parking lot. Even standing outside, she could hear the dull thunder of balls sent down a wooden lane and pins dropping. Music played from a jukebox.

She had just put her coins into the cigarette machine when someone yelled, "Cash! Tezhi! We got a city Indian in town. Cash, what are you doing here? Come on over and bowl a couple games with us," Bunk hollered at Cash.

Cash was tempted to run out to her Ranchero and head back to Fargo. She had never bowled in her life. Instead, she walked over to lane 5 and watched as Tezhi threw a black ball, a hundred times bigger than an 8-ball, down the wooden lane. The ball knocked over a bunch of white pins, leaving two standing on either side of the lane.

"A split! Let's see what you do now, hotshot. He's beatin' my ass. I can't bowl for shit. And he wants me to play on the Indian league with him." Bunk took a swig of beer. "Guess I'm good for a handicap." She must have been drinking for a while because she usually wasn't this talkative. "Just like in pool, huh, Cash? You wanna play? Come on, we got a pitcher of 3.2, and I think he paid for three hours. We still got another hour to go."

Cash shrugged. "I don't know how to do this."

"Good. Maybe I can beat your ass at bowling. Make up for all them shit pool games you beat us at. Come on." Bunk led her to a wooden counter. An older white guy was smoking, watching some soap opera on the TV. "What size shoes you wear?" she asked Cash.

Cash shrugged. Bunk put her foot alongside Cash's. "Let's try an eight and a half."

The counter guy passed over a pair of smelly gray and red shoes that, for all her lack of care and style, Cash would not have wanted to be caught dead wearing. Bunk grabbed the shoes for her and headed to a shelf of bowling balls. "Start with a lighter weight, maybe an eight or a ten. Just make sure your fingers don't stick."

Cash grabbed a ball, then put on the stinky shoes, while Bunk poured her a glass of beer.

"I don't know how to bowl," she repeated, taking a drink of the beer that was already warm and going flat.

"Just watch Tezhi. He's the one that knows how to do this."

The first time Cash tried to throw the bowling ball down the lane, it stuck on her thumb, thudded to the floor and into the gutter. Tezhi brought her another ball, same weight but with bigger holes. The next throw, she got down the lane and knocked over five pins.

Once she got the hang of it, Cash did all right. Tezhi won every game, sometimes scoring over two hundred. Cash managed to hang in there with scores over one hundred. Bunk not so well. With someone to compete against, Tezhi paid for another hour on the lane and two more pitchers of beer.

When their hour was up, they put the bowling balls away, took off the stinky shoes and stepped outside. Cash had come to DL to try to find the GED center, but, damn, it was already dark. Everything would be closed. Instead, Bunk and Tezhi talked her into following them back to Pine Point. "It's just up the road," she was told, and Bunk promised Cash her ma would have something cooked for them to eat.

Bunk's home was one of the HUD houses in the community where Geno had gotten directions to Jonesy's house. A dim light hung over a kitchen table with mismatched chairs. There was a hole in the sheetrock about the size of a fist over the couch in the living room, and the window had a

Southwest Indian geometric print bedsheet hung over it as a curtain. A blue and white yarn God's Eye hung over the couch. It touched but didn't cover the hole in the wall. Bunk's mom, loose strands of gray and black hair framing her deeply lined face, nodded hello when the half-drunk bunch entered her house. Without a word, she started to fry some hamburger. She boiled some macaroni, and shortly, there was a pot of hamburger hotdish on the stove. She set out four mismatched bowls and spoons on the table and retreated to one of the back bedrooms.

Halfway through the meal, there was a soft knock on the door. Bunk got up and answered. She talked to someone outside. She came back and told Tezhi and Cash there was going to be a tire fire over at Shell Lake. Her cousin wanted them to go. Cash tried to decline. "Come on, Cash," Bunk begged. "Come on. You too good for us, city Indian?" she teased.

Cash reluctantly agreed to go to Shell Lake.

THE NEXT MORNING, CASH WOKE up on Bunk's couch, staring at the hole in the sheetrock. She was fully clothed, and a blanket covered her. When she went to sit up, her head pounded. As soon as she lay back down, her stomach queased. She had to fight the bile that rose in the back of her throat. Everything about her smelled of burnt rubber and cheap wine. She didn't even know where the bathroom was. She rolled herself to sit upright, head in her hands. Sł figured that in six long steps she could make it to the door and outside. Which is what she did. She threw up as quietly as she could, leaning on the side of the house, watching the vomit hit the dirt. The rez dogs under the porch looked at her without a care.

Cash stood up and took a deep breath. Her Ranchero sat in the driveway. It looked no worse for wear. Thank God. Gingerly, she walked back into the house in search of a bathroom to pee. The first door she opened revealed Bunk and Tezhi wrapped around each other, dead to the world. The second was the bathroom.

When she got back to the living area, Bunk's mom set a cup of coffee on the table and motioned for her to sit and drink, then disappeared into the back of the house again. Cash drank and thought about the night before. She remembered driving to the lake and the acrid smell of the tires burning. She hadn't known any of the people there other than Bunk and Tezhi. They all laughed and joked. They shared whatever beer they had. Someone had brought out big green bottles of Spanada wine and passed those around. Then some Boones Farm wine.

Sometime during the night, Cash had found herself in the arms of some hunk of a guy. He'd kissed her on the neck and asked her where she had been all his life. Cash had laughed. The attention had felt good, even though his arm around her neck had been a little too tight. The smell of beer and cigarettes had filled the air around them as the guy tried to kiss her with his open mouth.

At that moment, Bunk had grabbed Cash by her arm and pulled her out of the guy's grasp. "Hey!" he hollered at Bunk.

"Go find another fish," Bunk hollered back at him.

"Geez, just sad, I can't leave you alone for a minute," Bunk said as she pushed Cash to sit down on a log away from the crowd. Bunk threw her arm around Cash's shoulders, more to steady herself than to hold Cash, then said, "That guy is bad news. Stay away from the Nodin boys. Ain't gonna let no friend of mine get snagged by him. Here, have a smoke on me."

They sat and watched the crowd standing around the fire as the flames shot up from the burning tires. Couples had their arms around each other. There were other groups of three or four folks all huddled together. Bursts of laughter erupted sporadically. Cash remembered noticing the guy who had tried to kiss her having his arm around another woman. *Easy come, easy go*, she'd thought.

"Come on, Cash, tell me what you were doing in DL. I ain't never seen you come around here. Must have a good reason. You can tell a sister." Bunk had said, interrupting her thoughts.

"Just some work."

"Like the work you were doing when you found them white girls who were being pimped in the Cities."

"Kinda."

"Kinda. Kinda. You like a female Billy Jack or somethin'? Kinda, kinda."

"Nah. Don't say that."

"Chill. I was teasin'. Come on. Tell me whatcha doing?"

Cash didn't know why, but she lied. "I was just driving around. On spring break. Didn't have nothin' else to do. No family to go to. Everyone seems to have left campus. Decided to drive this way for once. That's all."

Bunk passed Cash the bottle of Boones Farm she was drinking. "I hate this cheap shit, but a drink is a drink. Have some. You almost a cop and all. Did you hear about that girl from Devils Lake who got beat up?"

"No?"

"She ain't from around here. Devils Lake, I heard. She snagged one of the Nodin boys. The mean one. The brother of that guy who was all kissy with you. All the girls around here know to stay away from the Nodin boys. Heard he beat her up good. Heard she dumped him. Went back home. Can't hide anything from anybody 'round here. If you boogit, someone knows it."

"The guy that was kissing on me beat her up?"

"No, his brother. But the whole family is bad."

They sat in silence. Drinking.

"You know who else is gone, though?"

"No, who?"

"Nodin."

"Nodin?"

"Yeah. Kissy boy's brother. Can't remember his first name. Maybe once this wine is outta my system, I'll remember."

"What about 'em?"

"He snagged that woman. Beat her up. She's gone. He's

gone." She slurred her words. "We figure he followed her home to Devils Lake. If he was here tonight, there'd be nothing but fights. He's a real asshole."

That is where her memory of the night ended. Cash took a sip of coffee. She didn't remember coming back to Bunk's house and passing out on the couch. Damn wine. She couldn't recall that she had ever blacked out before. The coffee burned in her stomach. She pushed away from the table, rinsed out the cup in the sink and headed home. She needed a bath.

Back at her apartment, with the tire smoke washed out of her hair, Cash sat at her kitchen table playing solitaire. The blackout worried her. She still felt like she might throw up. She moved a couple aces and twos up, then shifted other cards around on the table. She thought about what Bunk had told her and what the women at the church had told her.

Everyone talked in circles. Like they really didn't know the whole story. That's how gossip worked. Like telephone tag. Everyone just had bits and pieces of the story. What Cash was able to glean from all of it was that there was a woman, by the name of Lori, who had been going to the church. The church women thought she was from Devils Lake, North Dakota. According to Bunk, there was a guy, her boyfriend, named Nodin—although no one knew his first name, everyone seemed to know he was the mean Nodin brother—who was gone now. He had a history of fighting, and he had probably jacked up Lori.

A chill ran up Cash's neck. The same kind of chill she felt when the dark figure stalked the graveyard. The same chill that crossed her body when her intuitive senses kicked in. There was something about the woman in the hospital basement and Devil's Lake, North Dakota, that felt right to Cash. She quickly switched some cards around. Moved another ace up. Set the rest of the deck down.

She ran down to the Ranchero and brought back a North Dakota state map. She spread it over the half-finished game of solitaire and used the little mileage scale on the side of the map to determine how long it would take to get from Fargo to Devils Lake. About three and a half hours. If she left from Ada, it might take her a bit longer.

As much as she dreaded the decision, Cash got in the Ranchero and drove to the county hospital in Ada. Of course, Doc Felix was there, a leer on his face as soon as she walked in through the basement doors. He didn't dare do anything like that around Wheaton, but with Cash on her own, he didn't bother to hide his awfulness.

Cash stood in the doorway, ready to run if he made any move toward her. "I need some piece of clothing or something from the woman you have here."

"Know something I don't?"

"None of your business, Doc. Just give me her shirt or something, okay? Wheaton can talk to you when he gets back." Lying, she added, "He called me this morning and told me to come pick it up."

Doc Felix gave her a look of disbelief but opened a drawer and pulled out a shirt. Laying on top of the shirt was a narrow-beaded bracelet.

"Give me both of them," Cash said.

"What do I get?" He leered.

"Stuff it."

"How do I know you're not gonna steal them?"

"Just give them to me. Let Wheaton know what I took." She quickly walked over to where he was standing, grabbed the shirt and bracelet and almost ran out of the room. Her steps echoed on the stone floor and stairs leading up out of the basement. Cash was afraid to look back, afraid the doc was right behind her. It wasn't until she was outside that she turned to make sure he wasn't back there. She was alone.

She laid the shirt and bracelet on the seat beside her, looked at the map one more time to get her on the right county road headed to North Dakota, and she took off.

Once in Devils Lake, she wasn't sure what to do. She stopped in a diner on the side of the highway and ordered a coffee and tuna sandwich. She was almost done with her meal and was mulling in her mind what to do when a tribal cop came into the diner. He was probably in his thirties and carried himself with the swagger of a vet who had seen combat and survived. His eyes slid around the room, checking for an enemy. Seeing no danger, he flirted with the teenage waitress. He called her honeybunch to make her blush before she seated him in the booth behind Cash. He reminded Cash of her brother. She took her last drink of coffee and stood up.

She stopped at the cop's booth. He looked startled but said, "You're not from around here. What can I do for you?"

"I'm from Norman County. Over in Minnesota. I work sometimes with the county sheriff, Wheaton."

"A kid like you? Come on, girl?"

"I'm not a kid. I do work with Wheaton. Help him out sometimes. He's out of town right now. He took a friend of ours down to Santa Fe to check out some art school they have for Indians. He's not back yet. But before he left, we got a body in our hospital that came in with the spring floods."

"Sit down." He motioned for the waitress to bring another cup of coffee. "Can I get you a piece of pie or something?"

Cash almost said no out of politeness but then said, "Blueberry."

After the waitress brought the pie and warmed up their coffee, he said, "Okay, tell me what this is about."

Cash told him about the body in the county hospital. About the woman who had washed in with the floodwaters and the county doc determining she had been hit on the head and then smothered. How Wheaton had sent her to the nearby White Earth Reservation to see if any women were known missing. Where Cash had heard two stories, one of a woman named Lori, originally from North Dakota, who hadn't been seen at the church she was attending since the flood. And then another story of a guy named Nodin—who was known for his temper. Everyone she had talked to said Nodin had a girlfriend from Devils Lake. She even told him about the woman's shirt and the beaded bracelet Cash had in her truck.

They finished their pie and coffee. The cop, who told

Cash his name was Richard, but everyone called him Dick, as in Dick Tracy, asked to see the shirt and bracelet. He led the way out after paying for both their coffee and pie. Cash showed him the items and told him she would need to take them back to Ada with her when she returned because they were evidence in the case in that county.

He held the folded shirt gently in his hands. He looked closely at the beaded bracelet. "Why don't you follow me to the station? Let me make a couple calls. You drove over here today? That's a long trek. Too late to head back. Why don't I see if the tribal office can put you up in the motel for the night? Might take me a couple hours to check this out."

Cash didn't know what to say. She had no plan but hadn't expected to spend the night in Devils Lake. "I can drive back."

"Nah, come on. Let us put you up. It'll be on the tribe's dime."

Once at the station, the first call he made was to the motel and reserved a room for her. Told whoever was on the other end the tribe would cover it. Then he brought her another cup of coffee.

Cash looked around the station. It was nothing like Wheaton's office at the county court building. This building was low and sleek, with lots of chrome and orange plastic furnishings. The jail cells were out of sight, probably behind the thick door with the big keyhole in it. Dick saw her looking around. "New building. Maybe five years now, maybe seven. I'm going to call over to Ada. There must be a deputy on duty, right?"

"Maybe."

Dick made the call. Chatted with whoever was on duty, who verified that Cash was who she said she was. Dick hung up and said, "Why don't you go to the motel, watch some TV or something, and I'll go see what I can find about all this, if anything?"

Cash was fine with that. She had just one experience of having to tell a family member that someone had died, and that was Geno's mother when his father was killed. She was relieved that Dick was the person who would check out this situation, and if need be, be the bearer of bad news.

Cash went back to the diner and got another pack of cigarettes. She drove through the small town of Devils Lake looking for a bar or liquor store but didn't see one. Her stomach was still upset. She swore to herself she would never drink wine again, but a beer would have hit the spot. Dry-handed, she returned to the motel, got a key to room 9 and parked the Ranchero right out front.

Inside, she listened to the bedsprings creak as she sat down on the bed. She had never stayed at a motel before. It kind of scared her. The parking lot was right out there. The window was just a window. Anyone could bust right through it. There was some kind of chain that went from the door to the doorjamb. Cash hooked it, but doubted it would keep anyone out if they were really determined to get in. She turned on the TV. With four channels to choose from, her choices were news, a variety show, and a show about a guy named Marcus. On the last channel, there was so much static she couldn't tell what the show was. She decided to watch *Marcus Welby, MD*.

Cash pulled the thin curtains shut tight, overlapping them some so no one could peek in. She pushed the lone wooden chair in the room under the doorknob as a secondary security measure. Feeling a little safer, she propped two thin pillows up behind her back, lay back fully clothed and watched TV.

A sharp rap on the door woke her. She jumped off the bed and pulled the curtain back enough to see who was out there. It was Dick. She wondered what time it was. The news was on—must be around ten.

She moved the chair away from the door and unhooked the chain. She knew from the somber look on Dick's face that he had found the owner of the shirt and bracelet. "Lori White Eagle," was what he said as he put the folded shirt on the end of the bed. "Her family wanted to keep the bracelet. I didn't have the heart to take it from them. I called the county sheriff's office in Ada and didn't get any answer this time."

"Wheaton is the only one there most of the time. He has that one deputy and a secretary, but the secretary only works during the day. I don't know about the deputy. Like I said, Wheaton's in Santa Fe. Took Geno down there to go to art school. He should be back the end of this week."

"So you're not an official deputy?"

"No, no, I just help out when Wheaton asks me to."

"Mind if I ask how old you are?"

"Twenty." Cash realized she was pretty good at lying all of a sudden these days.

"The family would like to go get their girl."

"As far as I know, they can. I don't know what the rules are. You must know. She's in the county hospital. In the basement. In Ada."

"The family said she just started to date a new guy. They met him once. Didn't like him."

"People where he's from, if it's the same guy, say he hasn't been around. And that he's really mean. No one's seen him since the flood. That's when we found her in the water outside of town. During the flood."

"What'd you say his name is?"

"Nodin. That's his last name. No one seems to know his first name. He has some brothers, but he's known as the mean one."

"Well . . ." Dick stood just inside the door, cold air coming in with him. "Guess I'll be going. S'pose you'll head out in the morning?"

Cash nodded.

"Well, the family appreciates you coming this way. It's hard news. Hard news," he said, looking out the door behind him as if they might be standing right there. "But they appreciate it. They'll go tomorrow to get the body. Give Wheaton my name. Tell him to call me when he gets back. Maybe he can track down this Nodin guy. Doesn't sound like someone a girl should mess with."

Cash shook her head yes.

"Well, good night. And again, appreciate you coming all this way."

After he left, Cash put the chain back on the door. She made sure the curtains covered the windows completely and lay back on the pillows on the creaky bed. The TV droned without her awareness of which show she had on. She must have dozed again because a door farther down the motel sidewalk startled her awake when it slammed shut and a man laughed. The TV was nothing but static, so she assumed it must be after midnight.

Cash peeked out the curtain and saw a couple cars and a pickup in the parking lot with her Ranchero. There was a motel sign by the road that read VACANCY in neon pink. She was wide awake, and the motel room gave her the creeps. She turned off the TV, left the lamp on the bedside table on and put the green plastic key chain with the gold number 9 on it on the bed. She hoped the motel owner had another key. Cash got into her truck and headed to Fargo. The only people on the road were 18-wheelers. The Milky Way shone across the sky. Stars glistened in the darkness. After a three-hour drive, cruising quite a bit over the speed limit, she crawled into her own bed and fell into a deep sleep.

Cash woke from a dreamless sleep. Without too much thought, she threw on a change of clothes and drove to Mahnomen. She told Debbi she found Lori's family. She asked her to keep an ear out for any information about the guy named Nodin, the mean one.

After a breakfast of scrambled eggs, toast and bacon, followed by a couple cups of good strong coffee, Cash got in her Ranchero and wound her way through the tamarack swamp roads until she found Jonesy's home on her own. Once again, Jonesy was waiting for her at the screen door of her house. She beckoned Cash inside and set a bowl of homemade stew in front of her. A plate of saltine crackers was also on the linoleum tablecloth accompanied by a cup of black coffee. They both ate in silence.

Their combined thoughts bounced off each other in the wood-smoked air of Jonesy's home. Cash thought about her trip to Devils Lake and the sadness that now engulfed Lori White Eagle's family. Jonesy thought about the healing sound of the wind through the pine trees that surrounded her home and the soft waters that ran in the stream a couple hundred feet back in the forest. The winds washed the sorrow from Cash's mind and the waters of the stream healed the ache in her heart.

Before she scooped the last spoon of stew out of her bowl, Jonesy said, "You know, that Boones Farm has formaldehyde in it. Embalming fluid. You're not dead yet."

Cash gave a short, sharp laugh.

"You have a few more things you gotta do here before you go that route."

"Well, I sure hope so."

"There are always things out there that will try to scare us, try to hurt us. Sometimes the darkness is real. It can be a message of what to stay clear of, what to avoid. Sometimes the darkness is our own fears. The best thing we can do is face our fears head on. You just have to keep your mind and heart on what you're here for."

"What do you mean, 'what I'm here for'?"

"You'll learn."

They sipped their coffee and talk switched to Cash's studies at school. Jonesy shared that she had never finished high school and hoped that Cash stuck with college. Cash shared how she hoped the weather stayed good so she could get back to doing field work. Jonesy invited her back to help her chop wood; there was a never-ending need, as Jonesy heated her home and also cooked on the woodstove. Cash promised to come help. Finished with small talk, which neither of them was very good at, Cash thanked Jonesy for the food and left. Jonesy stood in her doorway and watched Cash drive off.

Smoke filled the Ranchero cab and made its way out the slightly cracked open window on the driver's side. Country music sifted in and out of Cash's thoughts. The spring air was cool, even though the sun filtered through dense pine trees and stands of bare poplar. The swamp ground in places was still frozen; and if not, the water, still holding tree roots, cattail roots and other swamp plants, was freezing cold. The temperature was dropping as the sun headed toward the horizon, even though there were still hours of daylight left.

Cash didn't know what to do with herself. One situation was solved with Lori's body returned to her family. No one knew if Nodin was Lori's killer or not, although in Cash's mind he most likely was, and he would be in everyone else's mind too once they knew she was dead. Wheaton had only asked her to find out who the woman was who had washed up in the floodwaters—she didn't feel like it was her job to find Nodin. Maybe once Wheaton was back and he and Dick talked, they would go to work and find him.

Edie Birch, the woman buried up by Lake George, was killed in Hubbard County, not Norman County—Wheaton's area. And that brought Cash back to thoughts of the graves at the churchyard. The graves weren't Wheaton's issue either. He didn't know the graves existed, even if they were in Norman County. Therefore, they weren't Cash's issue either, but her curiosity and need to set things right nagged at her consciousness.

Cash didn't want to think about the dark shadow that haunted the graveyard. And Pastor Steene and his wife, Lillian, were a question also. Debbi, the waitress in Mahnomen, was sure Lillian was pregnant the few times she had seen her at the Five and Dime. But Cash had been to their home. There was no evidence of children. None. Not even a photo. There were the graves that the pastor said were their children's, but if Lillian had been pregnant and given birth, what happened to them? Why were they in graves and not running around the parsonage? And, dang, Cash slapped the steering wheel, did Wheaton really have a girlfriend? These thoughts all ran through Cash's mind as she drove back through the tamarack on deeply rutted roads that led back toward Mahnomen. She wasn't ready to head back to Fargo just yet.

Cash felt herself pulled to the church on the prairie. As she drove by, she saw the dark figure standing guard by the small graves. She gave it the finger and drove to the parsonage.

Lillian was outside, taking laundry down from the clothes-line. She was wearing a pale-yellow cotton dress that clung to her bare legs. Her feet were covered with rubber zip-up, fur-trimmed galoshes. Mud from the spring melt clung to the bottoms. The winter coat she wore was a dark brown everyday coat, not the coat she wore to the church services. Cash, who herself owned so few clothes, and then only what was necessary, was beginning to notice these things.

Cash got out of her truck and walked to the clothesline. Her tennis shoes sank an inch into the wet ground. The cold stung her feet. Cash helped Lillian take down the rest of the clothes and put them in the basket Lillian had hiked on her left hip. Still without a word, the clotheslines bare, Cash followed Lillian, who was carrying an armload of Pastor Steene's dress pants that didn't fit in the already overloaded basket, into the parsonage.

Once in the house, Cash removed her socks and shoes and Lillian set them in front of the floorboard heat vent. The clothes were cold as they began to fold them.

"Let me get you some coffee. Warm up a bit," Lillian finally broke the silence. "What brings you out this way? We're not having any services until Wednesday night."

"I went to visit a friend over at White Earth and just decided to stop by on my way home."

"Pastor Steene is off doing calls. Seems there is some kind of spring sickness going around. And then the women from the school at DL always want to talk with him. Get spiritual guidance." Lillian, in an uncharacteristic move, jutted out her hips and breasts as if to emphasize her last sentence.

"He must have a lot of people who depend on him."

"Yes, the devil's work is never done."

"How long have you lived here?"

"Too long. I think we're going to move soon."

"Really?"

"Yeah. John seems to do fine for a while, but then things get difficult. People want too much from him. God called him to reach the people. Save their souls. But too many people get involved in our personal life. Not many people understand that he's a man, just like them. We all get tempted. 'Thou shalt have no other Gods before me.' They put him on a pedestal. They don't understand his weaknesses. I'm his wife. I understand. 'What God has joined together, let no man, or woman'"—she looked deep into Cash's eyes—"'pull asunder.' Things get too complicated and then the Spirit moves us to another place. On to another group of needy women."

"Needy women?"

Lillian stared at Cash. "All those women from the GED center in DL. The last place we were, guess it was six years ago now. Where we lived before it was wayward girls from some mountain home where their parents sent them to have their out-of-wedlock babies. Drove me crazy. Crazy, I tell you. The pastor moved us here. To this peaceful prairie church. Promised me things would be different. But right away, he started to help the women at the GED center. And what's your need, Renee? What do you need from my husband?"

Cash was stunned by the turn of the conversation. Rather than respond to the direct question, which she had no answer for anyway, she asked, "Out-of-wedlock babies?"

"Sure. You know, parents whose good girls get pregnant by the football captain and they haven't finished high school? You know, those girls whose parents send them on 'spiritual retreat' or a 'year abroad'? Really?" Lillian *tsked*. "Those girls, more often than not, are pregnant, and the shame is too great for the parents to bear, so they ship them to some wayward home until the baby is born, and the baby is put up for adoption. Then the girl returns home to resume life as if a life never happened."

All the while Lillian was talking, she was rubbing her stomach in a circular motion. "Rachel in the Bible was barren. It was a cross she had to bear. God eventually blessed her with children. But first she had to share her husband with a servant girl. Another cross she had to bear. So many barren women in the Bible shared their husbands with servant women, who easily got pregnant. Harlots gave birth instead of the God-fearing wife. And the wife was made to take the child as her own." Her hands had forgotten to continue to fold clothes, and it was as if she had forgotten Cash was present too. "It's not always easy to be the wife of a man chosen to do the work of the Lord."

Cash avoided eye contact. She didn't know how to handle the turn the conversation had taken. She just kept sorting socks and folding the pairs in on themselves. White socks in one pile. Men's black dress socks in another.

"Do you have children?" Lillian, jerked back into the present, asked in an accusing tone.

"No. Do you?"

Lillian didn't answer. Instead, she shoved folded stacks of clothes into the basket and stomped upstairs. Cash stood at the table, drinking her coffee as she heard dresser drawers and closet doors slam shut upstairs. Then there was silence. The silence worried her. She was ready to go check on Lillian when she heard footsteps coming down the wooden stairs.

Lillian came into the kitchen wearing a bright pink, fitted, shirtwaist dress that flowed out from the belt cinched at her waist. Matching heels were on her feet. Three unbuttoned buttons pulled Cash's eye to her cleavage, the dress collar folded back toward her shoulders. Cash couldn't remember ever seeing a pastor's wife bare so much skin. Lillian stood in the kitchen doorway, hand on one hip, staring at her. Cash didn't move.

"Oh, my goodness, I forgot you were here. Slipped right out of my mind. You kinda scared me there for a minute. You look just like this Indian woman who was always coming here for 'guidance' a few months back. Scared me just now you did. Thought I was seeing a ghost. Say something. Move or something so I know you're real." Lillian's voice was no longer harsh. It sounded younger. If Cash had just heard the voice, not seen Lillian, she would have thought it was a teenager talking.

Cash took a drink of her coffee.

"Oh, good, you got coffee. I don't know when the pastor

will be getting home. Had some business over in DL, you know. Once he gets to talking with any of those poor, needy women in town, God knows when he will return. Did you want to speak with him?" She walked over to the kitchen counter, got a new cup from the cupboard and poured herself some coffee. Her back was to Cash.

"Lillian?" Cash was worried about the drastic change in Lillian's dress and appearance.

No response.

"Lillian?"

"Yes?" She turned around, her pale blue eyes looking directly into Cash's brown ones.

"Do you have any cream?" were the first words Cash thought to say.

"In the fridge. Help yourself. Whatever we have, we share with all the children of God."

Cash went to the fridge and poured a bit of cream into her coffee, although she usually drank her coffee black.

Cash sat down at the kitchen table while Lillian puttered around, wiping the counters, then putting a roast in a baking pan and into the oven. Cash was fascinated with how well Lillian maneuvered around the room in high heels, even if she did look a bit tipsy doing regular housework. Cash pulled her bare feet up under her crossed legs to warm them up.

"This roast should be done by the time he gets home. You want to watch TV or something while you wait for him? You're welcome to sit in the living room. Take your coffee with you."

Even though Cash had only stopped to help Lillian with her laundry, not to visit the pastor, she was curious, and a bit concerned now with the change in Lillian's demeanor. Cash decided to wait until Pastor Steene got home and then leave.

Cash went into the living room and knelt down in front of the TV console, which was bigger than the one Al had at his house. This solid, dark wood contraption had gold-colored knobs running down the right side of the box and silver antennae on top without tinfoil attached. She switched a button, and the TV turned on. It took a few seconds of gray and white static before a picture emerged. She switched between the three channels of ABC, CBC and NBC until she came across what clearly was a crime show, *The Mod Squad*.

Three misfits, working undercover, and a kindly cop as a mentor. *Huh, someone had put her life on TV.* Cash sat engrossed in the show. Sipping coffee until it was cold. Pots and pans were moved around in the kitchen and high heels clicked on the linoleum floor as background noise. Soon Cash was lost in the clamor of gunshots and a wild car chase happening on the screen.

A blast of cold air across her legs brought her back to reality as she heard the front door open and shut.

She overheard Lillian say to the pastor that Cash was in the living room and that she didn't know what "this young girl" wanted. The last few words were flung across the kitchen before they landed on Cash's ears. Cash jumped up and walked into the kitchen.

"Renee Blackbear. We sure are seeing a lot of you these

days. What brings your troubled soul to us today?" Pastor Steene asked, hanging up his wool overcoat on a peg beside the kitchen door.

Cash shrugged.

"Have a seat."

"I probably should get going. I was over by Pine Point to visit a friend and stopped on my way back to Fargo. Sorry to be a bother."

"Never a bother, girl." His face was a ghost in the steam that rose in front of his eyes as he took a sip of the hot coffee Lillian had handed him. He surprised Cash by asking, "Did you graduate high school with a diploma, or did you get your GED?"

"I graduated. Got my diploma."

"Good. Good. So many of your people seem to not know the value of a high school diploma. I just spent the afternoon at the GED center helping young women, young folks," he quickly amended, "with their practice test."

Lillian leaned her hip seductively on the kitchen counter. "Help. He's always such a good help with the young women. They just flock to him for the Lord's blessing."

Cash felt uncomfortable with the undertones that both of them were speaking in. She rinsed her coffee cup out in the sink and said, "Thank you, Lillian. I need to go. Head back before it gets too dark out."

"No need to rush. Stay. The roast is done. It will just take me a minute to get everything on the table."

Cash felt trapped. The man had pulled out a chair for h

and Lillian had quickly set three plates on the table as she talked. Cash, although uncomfortable, decided to eat a meal with them and then leave as quickly as possible.

Pastor Steene said a prayer, and they all dug into the roast beef and mashed potatoes. Once again, Cash was happy with the good food Lillian made. At the last meal, there had been questions and concern directed at Cash. This time there was silence as everyone focused on the food in front of them. As the pastor and his wife chewed their meal, Cash, who was trying to think of something to say to dispel the tension in the air, said to Lillian, "I was at the graveyard the other day and saw the two graves. I am sorry for your loss."

Pastor Steene's face darkened. Lillian went pale. She got up, the chair almost tipping over behind her, and threw her plate into the stainless-steel kitchen sink so hard that the plate broke, and pieces of mashed potatoes flew onto the floor. She stormed out of the kitchen.

"That was unkind," said the pastor. "Thoughtless."

Cash, stunned, finished chewing before she said, "I was trying to be thoughtful."

"The last baby died last fall. She is still grieving. As am I."

Cash didn't see grief on his face. What she saw was secrecy and anger that his holier-than-thou demeanor couldn't mask.

Cash heard doors slamming upstairs. A toilet flush. Dresser drawers opening and being shut loudly.

"Is she okay?"

The pastor didn't answer, just kept eating.

Cash heard footsteps come down the stairs. Lillian walked into the kitchen, wearing blue high heels, a short, bright red shirt-waist dress—the top three buttons undone. Her hair was up in a ponytail that swayed back and forth as she walked. In her arms, she was carrying torn pieces of the pink dress she had been wearing. She walked out the kitchen door. Cash looked at the pastor. He kept eating.

Cash watched Lillian through the window that faced the backyard. Her heels sank deep into the soft earth. Cash saw Lillian throw the dress into the trash barrel and set it on fire. Lillian stood there until the smoke and flames died down.

Cash had stopped eating, transfixed by what was happening in front of her. Pastor Steene finished his meal, drank his coffee and brought a plate of peanut butter cookies to the table, placing them in front of Cash. He poured them both a glass of milk.

Cash, who had grown up in foster homes, was used to crazy people. She had a foster mother who once threatened her with a butcher knife because Cash had missed a spot of egg yolk when washing a breakfast plate. Foster fathers who tried to rape her. Another foster mother who was strung out on some black diet pills the county doctor gave her. But this was a new level of crazy. Cash took a deep breath and was grateful the chair she sat on was on the side of the table with a clear and open path to the door.

Cash lit up a cigarette and took a deep drag.

The pastor got up and placed a green glass ashtray from the kitchen counter in front of her. Cash inhaled deeply a second time. Lillian came in from the backyard. She smelled like fire and burnt cloth. She smiled at Cash.

"Oh, good, John gave you cookies. I made them this morning. Did you get enough to eat?"

"Yes." Cash set down the cookie she was eating. She chewed slowly on the bite in her mouth. She kept both feet on the ground under the table, ready to run. "Are you okay, Lillian? Sorry if I upset you."

"I am fine, Renee—your name is Renee, right? And call me Lil. I am fine. The Lord in all his goodness watches over us." She sat down and grabbed the pastor's plate. She piled roast beef and mashed potatoes on it. She ate it all in big forkfuls, barely chewing it before swallowing. Then she ate four cookies, one right after the other. She reached over and grabbed her husband's milk and drank it down. She looked at Cash, cookie crumbs stuck to the pink lipstick she wore. "Children love these cookies. Do you love these cookies?"

Suddenly, Lillian jumped up from the table and rummaged through cabinets and drawers. She filled a green square Tupperware container with peanut butter cookies and set them in front of Cash. "Here, take these home. There are way too many for us to eat. I keep making double batches. I just can't seem to help it."

"Lillian! Sit down," Pastor Steene barked at his wife.

She sat, as if his voice struck her, her butt thudded on the kitchen chair.

He spoke to his wife with his hand on her shoulder in the monotone that made Cash feel drifty. "Let us pray. Yea, though I walk through the valley of the shadow of death, I will fear no evil . . ."

As he spoke, his wife's eyes glazed over, and she recited the words with him. Cash willed herself not to drift off with her. *What the hell is going on?*

When the recitation was over, Lillian got up docilely. She left her high heels under the kitchen table and cleared the supper dishes, then started to wash them in the sink. The man retreated to his study. He said he had to work on Wednesday evening's sermon.

"Let me help you with that, Lil." Cash grabbed a dish towel off a drawer handle and started to dry a plate.

"Lillian. Call me Lillian."

Once the dishes were dried and put away, Cash decided to get the hell out of there. The whole supper, burning of the clothes, praying and eating cookies had barely taken an hour.

"Thanks for supper, but I really gotta run. I have to go feed my friend's dog." Cash didn't know where that lie came from, but she needed out of the parsonage. She grabbed her socks and put them on. Her shoes. Her coat. She left the cookies on the counter. She muttered thanks as she left the house.

As Cash got into the Ranchero, the pastor reached out and put his hand on her back, between her shoulder blades. When she turned to look at him, his face was inches from hers. "It would be a blessing from God for me to be the one to bring you to salvation."

Cash jerked away and jumped in the truck. *Creep.* She

glanced back at the house; Lillian was standing in the doorway, bright red dress billowing out around her.

Cash looked at the man. He stood inches from her car door, hands hooked into his pockets now. She had forgotten to roll her car window up before she went to help Lillian with the laundry. The pastor's face shone in the light that streamed from the door his wife stood in. "Drive safe," he said. The steam from his breath entered Cash's space. "Come back tomorrow night for services. The women will have a potluck in the basement afterwards."

Even though the church and graveyard were a quarter mile away, Cash sensed the sinister presence of the dark form in the cemetery. In that same instant, as she backed out of the driveway, past the pastor's car, she heard a baby's muffled cry.

As she shifted from reverse to first gear, she leaned her head closer to the air outside the half-open window. Again, she thought she heard a faint whimper from inside the black sedan. The pastor walked rapidly toward his car. "I forgot my Bible," he called out to her. He opened the car door, reached in, and when he backed out, he held up a black leather-bound book. He stood by the car, Bible in hand, as Cash drove slowly away, the engine drowning out any sounds that might be heard. She headed toward Ada.

"Goddamn." Cash hit the steering wheel and kept driving. The house lights faded in the distance behind her. Everything behind her grew darker and darker. She could swear that was a baby she heard. Was there a baby? Or was it just the dark shadow playing tricks with her mind? Along with Lillian's strange behavior, and the man of God seeming to put the make on her, Cash didn't know what to think.

The farther Cash got from the parsonage, the more she doubted herself. Lillian must have lost the babies she was pregnant with and that is why she reacted the way she did. The pastor seemed to have all kinds of women coming on to him. Maybe he just assumed that is what everyone really wanted from him. Cash herself had been the recipient of too many men's advances who were supposed to be her protectors and weren't. That led her to wonder out loud to the air in the truck, "How am I supposed to know what is the right way for a grown man to pay attention to me? Maybe I'm just reading shit into this?"

Why the hell did Geno have to go to Santa Fe now? And where was Wheaton when she needed him? Cash smoked cigarette after cigarette. The country music, songs of lost love and beer, didn't drown the uneasiness that crept up her spine.

As she got closer to Ada, the traffic picked up. Dusty pickups passed her, often with a long-haired farm dog riding in the truck bed, ears blowing in the wind, their owners on their way into town to have a quick drink at the bar. It would be another evening where they could discuss the flood, the wet fields, the possibility of rain and when they could plant over a beer with friends.

Sedans came at her. With rural politeness, they dimmed their bright headlights as they approached. These were folks who were headed back home after a day of shopping in town or a visit to the doctor.

Near the outskirts of Ada her thinking got clearer. The dark shadow was not physical. She had heard plenty of babies in her lifetime. That sound coming from the pastor's car sounded like a real baby. Why would he leave a baby in the car? Why not bring it in with him? What was he hiding? When she hit the outskirts of Ada, she became determined to return to the parsonage and find out where that whining sound came from, but she had to admit to herself she was too afraid to go back alone. Drunks didn't scare her. Mean white boys didn't scare her. Farm girls with muscled biceps from throwing hay bales, drunk and jealous, didn't scare her.

But the dark shadow that patrolled the graveyard did. And, initially, Cash had thought Lillian seemed lonely, with her husband the center of all the attention. But her cattiness this evening had unnerved Cash. And while Cash was lulled by the pastor's concern in her direction for her salvation, that was his job, right? To save souls? And however much she wanted to believe his sincerity, the recent touches unnerved her more and made her cautious of his motives.

She drove aimlessly through Ada. Drove past the courthouse, the hospital. By Wheaton's house. Down Main Street and back. She sat in the cab of the Ranchero while the attendant at the gas station filled her gas tank. He seemed to remember her and checked the tire pressure without being asked. She drove down Main Street again. She wished there was a bar in Ada she felt comfortable stopping in for a drink—too close to Wheaton and people he knew. She drove by Wheaton's house again. In the yard, next to his house, sat

Gunner. His ears perked as if he recognized her Ranchero. She drove by, then did a quick U-turn. She needed someone to ride shotgun, may as well be Gunner, even if he hated her.

She stopped in front of the house, whistled and leaned over to open the door for him. Gunner ran to the Ranchero and hopped up onto the passenger seat. He looked at Cash as if to say, "See, I knew you'd need me sometime." And then the dog turned its face away from her and looked out the passenger window. He looked back one more time at Cash, as if to say this time, "Well, what are you waiting for? Let's go."

Cash headed back to the church. She drove first down the gravel road on the opposite side of the parsonage and looked at the graveyard and church across the plowed field from about a mile away. In the dark, it was just a silhouette against a starlit sky. There were no other farms along the church road for miles in either direction. John or Lillian would be sure to see the headlights of any car approaching. Cash was not about to park her truck a mile away and trek across a muddy field to scope out the situation.

She stopped on the road across from the graveyard, shut off the engine and rolled down the window. Cool spring air filled the truck. Silence surrounded her and Gunner. He looked toward the graveyard. His ears perked up and a deep growl sounded from his throat. The hair on the back of his neck stood straight up at the same time as Cash's arm hairs did.

She shivered, then pushed in the cigarette lighter and lit up. She held the cigarette down low in the car and bent over to take a drag. Her brother had told her of snipers who took out soldiers who were dumb enough to let the enemy see the tips of their lit cigarettes.

As she slowly blew the smoke out and watched it float out the passenger side window, she remembered another story Mo had told her. Of how, in the jungle, especially after a hard rain, the smell of cigarette smoke could tell the enemy exactly where your location was. The wind, the tiniest drift of wind, would carry the smell for a mile or more in the fresh air. Cash stubbed out the Marlboro, then immediately regretted it as she turned on the engine and headed on down the road. Before she'd even gotten twenty feet, she gave in and lit up another.

The longer she sat there smoking, the more convinced she became that she had heard a baby whimper in the pastor's car. What was he doing with a baby? If someone from the church had asked him to watch their child, why wouldn't he have just brought the baby in? Cash supposed he had seen her Ranchero and didn't want her to know what he was up to, but why would someone hide a baby?

"You know, Gunner, I wouldn't even have noticed, or even cared, if it weren't for those graves by the church. They make me nervous. It's what Wheaton means when he asks me, 'Wonder what you might think of this?' He's asking me what I know just by sensing it. It's the knowing. Sometimes it's just the knowing. I don't want it to be true. I really, really hope that cry was my imagination. I hope so."

She threw her cigarette butt out the car window. "Well,

Gunner, you up for a hike? You won't remember this, because it was before you arrived—we had a life before you, you know. Mo was home from 'Nam and he just walked up on those speed freaks who had those girls held hostage in that house down in St. Paul. He just walked up on 'em. Pretended he was drunk. Heck, for all I know, maybe he was drunk. So that's what we're gonna do, Gunner. Just walk up like we own the place, okay? Your job will be to bite any legs or arms you see coming at me, okay? Leave the baby to me. And then we run like hell if we have to. You got it?" Cash looked at Gunner as if he understood. And Gunner looked back, ears perked, excitement in his dark brown eyes.

Once the decision was made, Cash didn't hesitate. She drove directly to the parsonage and pulled into the driveway next to the black sedan. She refused to look toward the cemetery.

She expected Pastor Steene to come rushing out of his house to confront her. When no one appeared, she got out of the truck and reached for her .22. Then she remembered she had used all her bullets at target practice that one day at the county dump. She pushed the rifle back and stuck her car keys into her sock. She didn't want to have them fall out of her pocket. She didn't know why, but she felt like she needed to prepare for battle. She looked around behind the car seat and found a short Phillips screwdriver that she stuck up her shirt sleeve. All the while, she expected John or Lillian to come out and ask why she was back in their yard.

Cash quickly went around to the other side of the Ranchero

and let Gunner out. She reached up and turned off the dome light and left the doors open. She walked up to the house. Gunner at her heels. "Stay," she said.

Cash sauntered in as if she owned the place. She didn't try to be quiet; she expected to be stopped with each step into the parsonage. Neither Pastor Steene nor Lillian appeared. Cash looked into the living room. No one was there. The TV sat silent.

Cash headed toward the closed sliding pocket doors of the pastor's study. A sliver of light beamed on the hardwood floor. She heard muffled sounds coming from the room. She peered through the crack of the doorway. At first, her mind didn't grasp what she was seeing and hearing. John had Lillian on her back, legs splayed across the desk that he wrote his sermons at. Lillian, all but her legs, was buried in the red skirt of her dress. He jammed himself into her while reciting over and over, "Flesh of my flesh, seed of my seed."

When it finally registered what she was witnessing, Cash, without thinking, said out loud, "Well, goddamn," and, using all her strength, slid the pocket doors open. As they slammed loudly into the doorframe, Cash heard a whimper from the room across the hall behind her. Looking over her shoulder, there, laying on the floor in the opposite room, on a pink receiving blanket, was a black-haired, brown-skin baby. Cash had been so focused on the pastor and Lillian that she hadn't noticed the open door. In that second, Lillian scrambled upright, and Pastor Steene tucked himself rapidly into his pants. Red with rage, he advanced on Cash as Lillian pushed past her and grabbed the baby.

Still in shock from the scene she encountered, Cash was caught off guard when the pastor took two long steps across the room and grabbed her in a bear hug. Cash kicked and grasped whatever part of his clothing she could. At five two, she was no match for the six-foot-tall man.

Cash saw Lillian, flushed with her shirtdress unbuttoned, skirt past them with the baby clutched to her chest. The baby wailed. Cash kicked harder. Pastor Steene cursed her as he carried her, still in a bear hug, out of the study and down the hallway, into the kitchen.

"Lillian, open the basement door," he hollered.

Lillian came running, without the baby. As Cash struggled to get loose, she wondered where the baby was.

Lillian fumbled with the door but finally got it open. A blast of musty air hit Cash. As Cash was carried down the stairs she continued to struggle against the man. The damp smell of mold and old stone assaulted Cash's senses. At the bottom of the stairs, the pastor let one arm go of her while he still held her in a tight grasp with the other. Cash heard the sound of wood on wood and felt a blast of even colder air hit her body before she was thrown into a small, darkened room.

Cash landed on a stone floor. Her knee hit the ground and then her elbow before she could catch herself. A wooden door was slammed behind her, and she, again, heard wood on wood. In total darkness, she jumped up as fast as she could and limped in the direction of the sound. By feel, she found the coarse wood of the door. Even though she had heard the hasp lock, she still pushed on the door. There was little give. Cash heard the pastor walking up the basement stairs and the top door being shut and locked.

"Well, fuck judo," Cash said out loud and sat down in the dark, rubbing her knee and elbow.

Cash didn't know how long she sat there. She could hear occasional movement above her head, but guessed they must have moved to the upstairs bedrooms of the house. Every once in a while she could hear the baby cry. Sitting in the pitch dark, Cash pulled her knees up to her chest and rested her head on them. *How in the hell do I keep ending up in these predicaments? How in the hell do I get out of here?* was the next question in her mind.

"There is probably a light in here someplace," Cash said out loud. She figured she was in the root cellar, a cold space meant to store canned food and winter squash throughout the cold season. She gingerly crawled in the direction she guessed the door must be, while she tried to keep the pressure off the sorest knee. She found a pile of cold squash sitting in a corner. Judging by the shape, she figured it was Hubbard squash. As a farm girl, she knew that brand of squash could last all winter if kept cool but not freezing.

She reversed directions and used her right hand to balance while crawling and her left hand to feel the wall. She hit her head smack on the door before she found it again. Once there, she stood and flailed her hands around overhead. Aha! Her hand touched a string coming down from the ceiling. She moved her hand through the air again, this time more slowly. She found the string, grabbed and pulled. The lightbulb overhead blazed on and blinded her for a second.

Sure enough, there was Hubbard squash piled in one corner. The back of the cellar room was lined with canned goods: pickles, string beans, beets. Enough to last through a Minnesota winter. "At least I'm not going to starve to death."

Cash looked at her knee. It was scraped but not gushing blood. She figured her elbow would turn black and blue in a couple hours, but it moved just fine.

Cash listened for sounds from above. The pastor and his wife, with the baby, must be in the upstairs bedrooms. Cash started to pick at the door with the Phillips screwdriver that had somehow managed not to fall out when she was thrashing around, trying to get out of the pastor's grip. Just then, Cash heard footsteps advance toward the door at the top of the stairs. She reached up and shut off the light. When she heard the basement door open, she moved to the wall next to the door as quickly as she could. She gripped the Phillips screwdriver in her right hand, ready to pounce on whoever was there.

"Renee!"

Cash jerked. The pastor was right outside.

She stood silent.

"Renee! Where are the keys to that damn truck?" A slap on the door. "Answer me."

Cash leaned down and felt her sock. The keys were sitting in the arch of her left foot.

"Where are they?" He continued pounding on the door.

"I don't know. They must have dropped from my pocket when you were manhandling me upstairs. Or maybe they fell out by the truck in the grass."

"Bitch."

Cash leaned against the wall; adrenaline coursed through her veins. Her heart pounded so loudly she had to strain to hear his footsteps as he tromped back up the stairs. When he clicked the lock, she involuntarily jumped.

"Calm down, Cash. Think," she said. "Think." She steadied her breathing and willed her heart to slow. She could tell the entry door to the house opened and closed. Once again, she reached up, found the string and turned on the light. She shoved on the wooden door. It was built solid. Whatever lock was on there, it held tight, even after a couple shoves with all her body strength.

As she continued to push, Cash realized she was able to create a tiny crack between the doorframe and the door's edge. She could see where the door was locked. It looked like there was a piece of wood, almost like a painter's spatula but thicker, that when turned, slid into a metal slot.

"If I can get this screwdriver through this crack, I can probably lift that wood and unlock this door. Come on." Cash coaxed the door to open a bit wider. She heard Gunner make one loud bark and then silence. Then she heard the engine of her Ranchero turn over. "Goddamn, asshole. What did you do? Hotwire it? I'm gonna kill you, you do anything to my truck. Asshole."

She jammed the screwdriver through the crack. Frustrated, she realized all that did was create a round hole for the screwdriver to sit in. She pulled it back out and took better aim. This time, the screwdriver entered the door crack right below the wooden lock. She talked to the screwdriver and the lock. "Come on, baby, come on." Every once in a while she would stop to listen to the sounds coming from the house. All was quiet but the occasional muffled cry from way upstairs. "I'm coming to get you, baby. I am."

One last upward shove of the screwdriver and the door popped open. Cash fell with a *thud* out of the root cellar. "Damn!" She rubbed her knee. "Damn."

She glanced around the basement. The dim light from the root cellar fell on piles of boxes and tools of one sort or the other. The whole thing smelled damp and musty. *What if he comes back for me?*

Cash grabbed some gunny sacks that were sitting right outside the cellar door and laid them over the squash, then arranged them so it looked like someone had decided to cover up to keep warm. "Might stall him for a minute," Cash said as she patted the squash, then picked up her screwdriver.

She walked quickly to the bottom stair, counting her steps. It was a straight line. Nine steps. She went back to the root cellar and shut the light off, closing and relocking the door behind her. She walked in what she hoped was a straight line to the bottom stair.

They were closer than she calculated. She stubbed her shin and caught herself when she stumbled forward. After a few curse words, she started gingerly up the stairs, feeling her way in the dark. Finally at the top, she turned the doorknob and instantly remembered hearing the pastor lock it. Cash turned around and sat on the top step, elbows on her knees, chin in her hands. "Think, Cash, think." Once again, she listened for any sounds. She hadn't heard the man return, and she hadn't heard Lillian come downstairs.

What she did hear was a soft whimper that seemed to be coming from the foundation of the house. "Gunner!" He sounded like he was right next to her, and then Cash realized he must be close to one of the basement windows. "Stay right there, Gunner."

Cash sprinted down the stairs. She stumbled across the basement floor to return to the root cellar. She quickly opened the door and turned on the light. In its glow, which didn't quite reach to the darkest corners of the basement, she was still able to see a couple two-pane glass windows that sat around the base of the house. She focused on the one window that had a workbench underneath it. She held it in her mind's eye as she clicked off the overhead light and relocked the cellar.

Carefully, she made her way to the workbench. Crawled up on it. She heard Gunner scratching at the ground outside the window. She felt around its edges until she found a small metal latch on either side. After some twists and jabs with the screwdriver, the latches loosened. A burst of cold hit her in the face when she finally held the window in her hands.

"How am I going to get this back on here, Gunner?" she

softly asked the dog while she worked to push the screen out onto the ground. Gunner licked her hands and face.

"Go on, dog. Geez, don't slobber all over me," she whispered. She slid the glass window out on top of the broken screen, far away enough that she wouldn't break it crawling out. She bent down and reached around in the dark until she found a metal can that seemed strong enough to hold her weight. She used that to stand on to push herself up and out.

"Thank god I'm skinny, huh, dog?" she said softly as she rolled on the lawn. When Gunner whimpered with happiness, she said, "Shhh. I gotta get this window back in."

With the window back in place, Cash moved quietly along the side of the house, Gunner slunk beside her, until she could see where the pastor's car was parked. Her Ranchero was gone. Her heart sank. "What the heck? Where in the hell would he take my truck?" She grabbed Gunner's neck, feeling the threat of tears tighten her throat. "Why my truck?"

She moved farther away from the house to look up and down the gravel road. From her vantage point, she could see the headlights of her truck pointed at the graveyard down by the church. There was something moving in the graveyard. A human figure. Not the dark creature she had been seeing. It was the pastor, and it sure looked like he was digging with a shovel.

"We should leave, Gunner. We should get the hell outta here." She watched the pastor. He bent forward, then up, and threw dirt with a long-handled shovel. "I don't know if he is digging that grave for me or the baby, but we gotta get the baby, Gunner."

Cash moved back to the side of the house where she would not be seen or cast a shadow if a car did happen to drive by. "What am I going to do? What's the plan of action?" she asked as she gripped the fur at the dog's neck.

"Okay, we're going in. I'm going in. You stand guard and bark if he gets back before I get out of there with the baby. Got it? We got a plan, dog?"

Cash patted Gunner's head and headed for the door of the house. Once inside, she bounded up the stairs, not caring if Lillian heard her coming or not. When she reached the top, she noticed one of the rooms had a door open, light streaming out into the hallway. Cash walked directly to that door.

Lillian sat in a rocking chair. A small bundle wrapped in a pink blanket was cradled in her arms.

"Renee. Did you come to see the baby? Look at her. Don't you think she looks just like John?"

Cash didn't recognize the woman's voice as Lillian's. It had a kinder, more maternal tone. Lillian's face glowed. There was a softness to it that Cash had never seen. Wary, but curious, Cash took a step into the room to take a closer look at the baby's face. She saw no resemblance to the white guy at all. It was an Indian baby. Beautiful brown skin. Thick black hair that stuck straight up. A two-inch mohawk hairdo on a newborn. Cash couldn't help but smile.

"I don't know, Lillian, her skin is pretty dark."

"Lily. People always confuse me with Lillian. Isn't she beautiful? We finally got a girl."

"This is your baby, Lillian?"

"Lily." The woman, who gently held the baby, gave Cash a sharp look. "John told me, 'Flesh of my flesh, seed of my seed.' He says that about every baby he brings home. This is our baby. Look, she has his eyebrows. And that thick swatch of dark hair. The spitting image of her dad."

"Where are the other babies, Lily?" Cash decided to go with the current situation.

"Oh, Renee. I thought they were ours. John said they were ours. He wants me to be happy. But all they did was cry. Lil hates when they cry." The woman who called herself Lily gently put her hand over the baby's mouth. "Lil put them to sleep. She put them to sleep for a long time."

Cash didn't dare move. And who the hell was Lil?

"Look how peaceful she is. Not a peep out of her," Lillian said, moving her hand away from the baby's mouth. "She's been quiet like this since John left. Do you know where he went?"

"I think he's at the church."

"He's probably giving thanks to the Lord for the abundance of His gifts."

"Can I hold the baby?"

"Oh, I don't think that's a good idea, Renee. Babies need their moms."

How am I going to get this baby without hurting her? Cash asked herself. She needed to do something fast.

"We could go downstairs, and I could get you a cup of coffee or tea? A little bite to eat? You must be hungry. Babies are a lot of work."

"That would be nice." Lillian stood up and clutched the baby to her chest. She wore the same dress that had been hiked up around her waist down in the study. She was barefoot, and her hair was disheveled. Lillian had the same glassy-eyed look and slow movements as the veterans Cash had seen on leave from Vietnam.

"Are you okay? Do you want me to carry the baby down the stairs? You look a little tired?"

"No. No. I got her." Lillian clutched the baby tighter. Cash backed away.

"Let's go downstairs and get some food in you. Build up your strength. I've heard babies keep you up all night."

Once downstairs, Lillian sat down on one of the wooden chairs at the kitchen table while Cash rummaged in the fridge and cupboards and found the fixings for a roast beef sandwich. She set the plate of food in front of Lillian, who was still transfixed on the baby. She cooed and baby-talked to the infant, all the while proclaiming how much she looked like John.

"Do you want some milk? Or tea?"

"I'll take some coffee. You're right. I'll probably be up all night. We've waited so long for a baby."

Cash listened intently to the sounds outside the house. Gunner was quiet, and she didn't hear her truck or the pastor. "What happened to the other babies?"

There was a flash of anger in Lillian's eyes, and her voice changed. "You should keep talking to Lily. She already told you I hate hearing babies cry." Lillian squeezed tightly, and the newborn whimpered, almost as if she knew better than to make a louder sound. The expression on Lillian's face changed abruptly.

"I told you, I'm Lily, call me Lily. Lil hates when babies cry." She took a bite of her sandwich, then went back to cooing at the baby.

I have entered the Twilight Zone, Cash thought. A story from the TV show ran through her mind. It was an episode where a young girl crawled under her bed to chase her dog and both of them went through the wall into the fourth dimension. *I have entered the fourth dimension.* Cash watched Lillian and the infant out of the corner of her eye while wiping non-existent crumbs off the countertop. *How do I get the baby?*

A low growl outside the kitchen window over the sink alerted Cash to dull footsteps coming up the entryway. Instinctively, she grabbed the first object in reach. *A stupid butter knife.* But she kept it clutched in her hand all the same, her back to the counter.

The pastor's dark shadow filled the kitchen doorway. "What the hell are you doing up here?" Behind his physical body loomed an even darker shadow.

"Oh, John, don't be rude to our guest. She's helping with the baby. She made me a sandwich and a cup of coffee. In case the baby keeps me up all night."

The pastor, while keeping his eyes on Cash, walked to Lillian and the baby. The shadow followed. A chill filled the room, and it wasn't just from the door they left open behind them. To Cash, it looked like cold steam rose off the dark shadow. She backed herself against the kitchen counter, as far from it as she could get. Pastor Steene patted his wife on the head. The look he gave the newborn was calculating. The baby's eyes grew wide. Where the infant had squirmed and moved occasionally in Lillian's arms, the baby's whole body now went still. *She looks like a rabbit that has frozen all movement, thinking, hoping she won't be seen by the hunter,* Cash thought.

The scraping of a chair across the linoleum made Cash jerk. She glanced at the shadow. It hadn't moved. Pastor Steene snorted a laugh. "May as well make me a sandwich. I have a long night ahead of me too."

Cash didn't move.

"Now!" Pastor Steene snapped.

Cash moved sideways to the refrigerator. She didn't dare take her eyes off the man or the shadow. Her gaze skittered back and forth between the two, keeping her awareness on both. She quickly grabbed the leftover roast beef out of the fridge and some mustard. When it was ready, she took a step toward the table and slid the plate across, making sure she stayed out of arm's reach.

Cash jumped when Pastor Steene pushed back from the table and went to the basement door. When he turned the handle and realized it was still locked, he turned to Lillian. "Did you let her out?"

"Let her out? What would she be doing in our basement? I was upstairs with the baby, and she just came up to help me."

"How did you get out?"

"John, stop being so rude. How did she get out of where? She came to help me." To Cash, she asked, "Are you the one who gave birth to my girl? I thought Edie did that? John said he brought the baby in the car. He's never brought the baby's mom before."

Pastor Steene quickly returned to the table and moved his chair closer to Lillian's, leaning in to speak softly, almost in a sing-song voice. "Hey, isn't she pretty? Look at that hair. Just like mine." He swept his dark brown hair back off his forehead.

The shadow seemed to fill more of the doorway.

"This is my child," he said pointedly in Cash's direction.

Cash stayed stuck to the kitchen counter. *These folks are crazy. Like, really crazy.*

"Whose baby is that, John?" Cash dared to ask. She needed verification from him as to what Lillian had already said to her.

"Mine. Flesh of my flesh, seed of my seed. And really none of your business, but since you've come poking around in the doings of God's work, you've now made yourself *my* business."

"God's work? Taking babies? Killing babies? Your wife killed two babies already. And you buried them in the church graveyard?"

The shadow seemed to grow darker as the talk continued.

Lillian looked frantically between the pastor and Cash. "Killing babies? We didn't kill any babies." Her voice took on an accusatory tone. "Lil hates when babies cry. And Lillian doesn't understand the ways of the Lord. She says she does, but she doesn't. Men in the Old Testament had many wives. Their servant wives gave birth to children and were brought into the bosom of the family." She gently rocked the baby, brushing its hair with her free hand. Cash couldn't help but think that the baby was laying so still, tolerating the touch, waiting for rescue.

Yeah, baby, I'll figure something out.

"What is *Lily* saying, John?"

"Shuttup, you stupid bitch," he said to Cash.

Lillian grabbed his forearm as he started to rise. "Stop, John. Don't swear around our baby. Renee has just come to help. Stop fussing, you're going to upset the baby."

"Where did you get the baby, Lillian?" Cash asked sharply, her need to know overriding her fear.

Lillian quickly stood up, glaring at Cash, then shoved the baby into Pastor Steene's arms and stormed out of the room and up the stairs.

"Now look what you've done," said Pastor Steene.

"What I've done? What have *you* done? What are you doing with this baby?" His face darkened with anger at Cash's questioning. She glanced again at the shadow. It was still there, filling the air with darkness and cold. The baby lay as still as death in his awkward arms. Cash pictured him at the graveyard, digging.

Both of them turned as footsteps echoed on the wooden stairs. When Lillian, Lily, Lil, whoever she was, re-entered, her hair was falling in loose waves over her shoulders. Cash was surprised to see that she had changed clothes. Now, she was wearing a pale blue cotton dress with buttons up the front—this time, only the top two were left unbuttoned.

"My goodness, John, you can't hold a baby like that." Lillian reached out and took the baby from his arms. Laying the baby's head on her shoulder, she stood right by John's chair. She pat-pat-patted the newborn's back.

"Shh. Shh. Shh," she whispered, although the baby wasn't making any sound whatsoever. Cash could see Pastor Steene's mind working. *He must be trying to figure out what to do with us all*, thought Cash. When she caught a glimpse of the baby's face, she could see her eyes were wide open, as if searching the room around her. If a baby could look worried and cautious, this one did.

"Lillian," Cash spoke tentatively, not exactly sure who she was speaking to at the moment, "maybe the baby wants some more of her bottle. Should I warm up some milk for her?"

"Yes, yes. As long as you're here to help."

Cash quickly grabbed the baby bottle off the kitchen table, filled it with milk from the fridge and put it in a pan of water on the stove. She maneuvered as best she could without putting her back to the couple, or the shadow that lingered by the door, for a second longer than she had to. The man kept a wary eye on her and his wife.

When the bottle of milk was warmed, Cash set it on the table. "Here."

Lillian sat back down and asked Pastor Steene, "Can you shut the door? The baby is going to catch a cold." He backed his chair away, walked backward to the door, closed it without taking his eyes off Cash and returned to sit by his wife.

Cash scanned the room for a weapon, any weapon other than the butter knife she still held in her hand. She grabbed the damp dishrag and took a swipe at the table where they sat and grabbed the empty plates in the process. She moved quickly out of the man's reach—it seemed he was being careful not to upset his wife. Cash put the dishes in the sink, then opened a drawer. It didn't contain silverware.

"The silverware goes in the next drawer." Lillian looked up briefly. The pastor glared at Cash, and she pointedly kept her eyes on Lillian and the baby. Finally, the pastor looked at them to see what Cash was staring at.

Cash quickly pulled open the next drawer. It not only had silverware; it had a paring knife. She exchanged the silverware for the short knife. Not a good weapon, but better than a butter knife. Neither seemed to notice what she was up to.

"You can't just take a baby."

"You and your kind. Having babies left and right. Some don't even know who the fathers are. They come to me, praying for forgiveness. To get washed in the holy water of forgiveness. Loose trash. Leave your babies to be raised by some relative while you gallivant through the streets of these small towns. Lily needs someone to care for. Someone to calm the devil's spirit that roams in the depths of her soul."

"Lily needs someone to care for?" Cash was incredulous. "That baby needs its mom."

"Her mom? Lily is her mom."

"Who gave birth to her?"

"Don't be stupid. That person is long gone." Lillian looked up. "Lillian was jealous about Edie carrying our baby. She *is* our baby. Flesh of his flesh, seed of his seed." Then returned her gaze back to the newborn.

"You can't just steal other women's children," Cash said sharply. She glared at both him and the darkness, which seemed to have moved closer into the room, closer to the pastor.

"I heard they had the mother's services just the other day up by Lake George," said Pastor Steene. "I'll be doing another private service before the sun comes up." He looked her up and down. "I am pretty sure I dug deep enough and long enough."

Cash locked eyes with him. *No way in hell,* she thought. The darkness at the door had moved farther into the room. She was sure of it. *And fuck you too.* The air in the room got colder, followed by a stench that smelled like a combination of dog shit and rotting leaves.

Between the fridge and the table, a clear mist filled the space. Cash saw Jonesy putting some wood into her stove, the heat emanating from it wrapped around Cash. Jonesy looked her directly in the eyes and said, *That thing feeds on fear.* Jonesy faded as fast and silent as she had appeared.

I am in the fourth dimension, Cash thought again. She looked directly at the dark shadow. *Yeah, well, fuck you too. Go to hell. Go back to wherever the fuck you came from.*

As soon as the words were out of her mind, the thing grew and filled more space in the kitchen.

Cash took a deep breath. She stilled her heart. Stilled the fear that threatened to course through her body. She advanced on the shadow. With each step, the shadow became smaller. Cash willed the thing to die. As soon as she thought the word *die,* the creature started to evaporate, like a balloon losing air. Gunner howled outside.

The pastor jerked around in his chair and looked toward the door. Nothing was there. He whipped back around and started to get up.

Without thinking or planning it, without even a clear aim, Cash grasped the tip of the paring knife and sent it flying through the air directly at the pastor.

It stuck solidly in his neck. As he pulled the knife out, he screamed, "I'm gonna kill you," and his blood spurted across the kitchen table.

When he fell to the floor, Lillian screamed. Cash rushed to her and grabbed the baby from Lillian's arms, then ran.

As Cash passed the sedan, she sensed more than saw Gunner, ears and tail up, standing on guard. She headed toward the church. Without any farm or yard lights around, she used the dim light from the quarter moon overhead to make out the outline of the road. She didn't think. She didn't have a plan. She just knew she had to get as far away from the house as possible.

Behind her, there was a blood-curdling scream. Lily? Lil? Lillian? Cash kept running, gasping for air. And then she heard it—feet on gravel gaining from behind.

Fear propelled her forward faster as she imagined the pastor coming after her. Cash turned her head to look. It was the woman. Her mouth in an open scream. Her hair flying behind her. The skirt of her dress riding almost to her hips as her long legs pumped her forward ever closer to Cash. Cash forced herself to run harder, to increase the distance between them. Gunner kept pace beside her.

When she turned down the gravel driveway of the church parking lot, she saw the woman had gained ground. Cash ran around to the front of the truck and shoved the baby under the cab between the two front wheels. "Watch her, Gunner," she yelled as she ran toward the graveyard. Gunner crawled under the truck. Lillian kept chasing Cash, and every once in a while Cash could feel Lillian's fingertips brush her back or shoulder.

Cash charged toward the only weapon she could see: the shovel stuck in the ground. Just as she was about to reach it, Lillian grabbed Cash's braid and yanked it back. Cash stumbled but didn't hit the ground. The judo training kicked in. As Lillian pulled, Cash followed the tug. She used her full body weight to knock Lillian to the ground. Cash landed on top of her and scrambled off, but Lillian grabbed again for her braid and caught it. Cash slammed her knee, with all her body weight, down on Lillian's wrist, causing her to scream. Cash removed herself from Lillian's grasp, jumped, then kicked her in the side. Lillian rolled into a fetal position, her face contorting. Suddenly, as if with superhuman strength, Lillian sprang to her feet and lunged at Cash, her hands like claws went straight for Cash's face.

Cash jumped backward, then quickly stepped forward. Lillian tripped and fell face-first into the ground. She rolled over, curled in a ball, crying. The cries changed to a whimper and when she looked up at Cash and said, "Give me my baby. I thought you came to help me. I want my baby," she sounded like Lily.

"That's not your baby."

The woman on the ground contorted. Her back arched and the skin on her face tightened. In a voice Cash now recognized as Lil's, she rasped, "She's ours, bitch." Within seconds, she lunged at Cash. Cash was caught off guard by the sudden change in Lillian . . . and her strength. She was taller than Cash, with longer limbs. None of Cash's judo kicks reached her. Cash retreated, backed away to get out of her reach. Lillian . . . Lil circled her. She was like a cat stalking its prey.

"He planted his seed in all of us. The baby is ours. We married him. Edie fornicated with him. She thought John would let her come live with us."

Cash turned in circles, moving ever closer to the shovel. "How did you get the baby?"

"The baby was jaundiced, and the hospital kept her. Edie

came to the house, thinking we'd take her right in. Lillian got rid of her right quick."

"How did you get the baby?" The shovel was almost within reach.

"When Edie didn't show back up at the hospital to pick up the baby, John said he would call on the grandparents. He went back a few days later, and the staff let him bring the baby home. He told them he was taking the baby to her grandparents."

"And what about the two babies buried here?"

"We put them to sleep. They wouldn't shuttup."

With Lillian distracted, talking, Cash saw an opportunity, turned quickly, grabbed the shovel with both hands and swung with all her might. It caught Lillian in her midsection, then Cash brought the shovel back and hit Lillian square on the head. She fell limply to the ground.

Cash held the shovel like a baseball bat, ready to strike again if Lillian rose from the ground. When she didn't move, Cash poked the body with the tip of the shovel. She still didn't move.

"Gunner. Come here."

Gunner ran over.

"Watch her. If she gets up, bite her, okay?"

Gunner sat by Lillian, his tongue hanging out the side of his mouth.

Cash walked backward to the truck, not taking her eyes off the woman. Gunner didn't move. Cash bent down and took a quick look at the bundle under the cab, just lying there. The

SINISTER GRAVES · 179

baby had gotten loose from the blankets and was sucking on one of her hands. "Come on, kid. It'll be a bit warmer in the truck." She pulled her out and rewrapped her as best she could, then laid her on the passenger seat.

Cash walked to the back of the truck and grabbed some loose pieces of twine that lay there. Each piece, which at one time had held a hay bale together, was about five feet long. Cash figured they would work to tie Lillian up, which is what she did. Hands behind the back. Feet together. Lillian was alive, but not conscious. She groaned a couple times as Cash wound the twine around her wrists and ankles, but that was the extent of her alertness.

"I don't know, Gunner. You think she can get out of that? No? I don't think so either. She's tied up pretty dang good. I don't know how long before someone will come to get her. I'm going to grab a blanket, though, to cover her up with. It's kinda chilly out here. What'dya think?"

When the dog didn't answer, Cash got an old army blanket from behind the seat. She went back to Lillian, who was still out cold, and laid it over her.

"Come on, Gunner. We're outta here. Come on."

Cash once again walked backward to the truck. Gunner crawled in and sat on the floor, head resting on the seat next to the baby.

Cash got in and locked both doors just in case. She had had enough surprises for the night. "I'm not taking any chances, Gunner. Hope the pastor doesn't rise from the dead. You be ready to rock and roll if I need you. You hear me?"

She reached into the glove box and found a book of matches. "Oh God, I could use a cigarette. And a beer. Fuck that, a twelve pack." She lit a match and looked at the mess the pastor had made of the wires under the dash in order to hotwire her truck. "I hope all he did was hotwire it." She pushed in the clutch and the brake and touched two wires together. The engine turned over. "Hallelujah! Praise the Lord. Sorry, Gunner, I think I might be a little crazy myself here. Let's get outta here."

She flicked on the headlights. Lillian was still on the ground. She put the truck in drive and did a half-circle on the church lawn and got the hell out of there.

She lit up a cigarette, rolled down the window and blew the smoke out as she spoke. "Where's your owner, Gunner? I'm gonna have to find a different cop to help me out here. Let's go to Mahnomen. I'm not driving to DL tonight." She leaned down and reached under the seat and felt around. When she didn't find the bottle she was looking for, she said, "Guess I shouldn't drink with a baby in the car on our way to talk to some cops, huh, Gunner?" She took a long drag of her cigarette. "Why the hell am I talking to a dog? A dog who doesn't even like me?" She reached over and did a half-hearted pat on the dog's head. "You did good for a mutt. And what about you, baby? How are you doing?" She slid the blanket below the baby's chin. "I don't have a clue what one does with a kid. You okay? Just cry or something if you're not, okay?" Cash blew more smoke out the window.

Cash could see the streetlights of Mahnomen up ahead.

Thank god. She pulled into a parking spot in front of the courthouse, which also served as the jail. A lone light shone through the doorway at the top of the marble steps. She picked up the baby, brushed the mop of black hair and looked into her dark eyes. "Come on, baby. Let's find some place safe for you." She told Gunner to stay and walked into the jail.

The night deputy, who was still engrossed in the Zane Grey novel, jumped to his feet when he saw Cash walk in. "What the hell happened to you? Car accident? Get over here. Sit down. Is your baby okay?"

Cash didn't understand his excitement or concern until she caught a glimpse of her reflection in the glass door across from where he was sitting. Her face was smeared with dirt on one side. Her long braid had wild strands sticking out all over. There was a rip in her jacket sleeve where the pointed end of the Phillips screwdriver was sticking out. She had totally forgotten she had shoved it up her sleeve back there in the basement.

Out of habit, she pushed the screwdriver back into the arm sleeve and dropped into the chair he pulled out from behind his desk. The baby started to wail. Cash put the infant's head up to her shoulder and patted her back like she had seen Lillian do. The wails shifted to a whimper.

Cash blurted out the whole story to the deputy, minus the dark shadow incident. He half stood, feet planted a bit more than shoulder-width apart, his butt rested on the wooden desk. To Cash, he looked like the thirty-year-old son of any Scandinavian farmer in the area. His face registered disbelief.

A couple times he shook his head "no" in doubt, but when she stopped to take a breath, he motioned with a calloused, thick hand, a gold wedding band on his ring finger, for her to continue.

When the baby began to cry again, the deputy said, "You wait here. I'm gonna run down the street and get my wife. It's just a couple blocks. She'll know what to do with the baby. Stay put." And he took off out the door.

"Shhh, shhh, shhh." Cash stayed on the wooden chair and rocked the baby until he reappeared with his wife. Her blond hair, which earlier in the day must have been a teased hairdo, was now sticking out all over. She, too, looked like farmer stock. She probably had been in bed and put on whatever pair of pants and shirt were handy. Everything was wrinkled. But she had a baby bottle in one hand, filled with milk, and a handful of cloth diapers in the other.

"Oh, my goodness. You poor thing." She took the crying baby from Cash's arms, cradled her deftly in the crook of her arm and gave her the bottle. The baby sucked hungrily.

"Go ahead. Finish your story," the cop said to Cash.

"Nothing more to tell. That's it." Now that the baby was safe, Cash felt a wave of exhaustion. "I'm tired."

"But you think the pastor is dead, and you left his wife tied up in the graveyard?"

"Yes."

"You can't go anywhere until we get this checked out, you know? The only place I got to put you is a cell."

"Huh," Cash said. *It won't be the first time.*

"Come on. I'm not gonna lock the door. Go ahead and lay down. Just lay down. Or sit here until I get back. It's not much, but it is better than that hard chair out there."

Cash sat on the thin mattress in the cell. She heard his wife as she baby-talked to the baby. Cash heard the crackle of his walkie-talkie as he called in another deputy. She leaned against the brick wall and immediately fell asleep.

CASH AWOKE TO THE MUFFLED sounds of men's voices. Every muscle in her body hurt and she stabbed herself in the hand with the screwdriver when she went to rub her arms. She pulled it from her jacket sleeve and stuffed it in her back pocket. She rolled her head to loosen her neck muscles, which were stiff from being flopped over against the brick wall. The cell door was still open, so she walked toward the voices.

There were now five men in uniform at the desk. They all got quiet when she stepped out of the cell area. Three wore county uniforms and two were tribal deputies. Cash could see out the front door. The sun was up. She nodded to the men that she was headed to the women's restroom down the hallway. They nodded back.

After using the toilet, she looked at her reflection in the mirror over the sink. She ran water until it was hot and splashed some on her face, washing away the tiredness and dread. The fear and the sorrow. She redid her hair into one long smooth braid down her back and brushed off as

184 · MARCIE R. RENDON

much dirt as she could from her clothes, then walked back to the five men who stood around the front desk.

The guy she had first talked to when she arrived at the station said, "I'm Deputy Bjerke. Didn't get a chance to introduce myself last night. And you are?"

"Ca . . . Renee Blackbear. Are they alive?"

"He isn't. She is. We had an ambulance take her to the hospital in DL. She probably has a skull fracture. You gave her a pretty good whack with that shovel. I need you to tell us again what happened. I've called the secretary in; she should be here any minute. Might be faster if she typed it up while you tell them what all happened. That all right with you?"

"I guess. Where's the baby?"

"My wife took her to our house. She'll take care of her until we get this sorted out."

Cash nodded and followed him and two other deputies into a back room. They all took wooden chairs at a big oak table. When the secretary arrived, someone brought in a typewriter and a stack of paper.

"Go ahead. Maybe start with where you thought you heard a baby in the car last night and what you did from there on." Cash retold the events of the previous night. Midway through the story, one of the men got up and left the room. Deputy Bjerke asked Cash to wait up. The man returned with four cups of hot coffee, two to a hand. He set them down on the table, left and came back with another cup that he placed by the typist. He also put down a bowl of sugar cubes and a carton of milk.

"Go ahead," said Deputy Bjerke.

Cash continued her story.

"And then I drove here," she finished and took a sip of her lukewarm coffee, then lit a cigarette. One of the tribal cops pushed a metal ashtray across the table to her. They all stared at her when she didn't have anything more to say.

Then they started asking questions. Where did she live? What did she do for work? Who were her parents? How old was she? They asked her to repeat parts of the story. What did she study at school? Was she drinking last night? One of the men asked, "You said you threw the paring knife across the kitchen and that it stuck in the guy's neck? That takes some skill to throw a knife like that and kill a man."

For the first time since they started questioning her, Cash felt fear. "I didn't mean to kill him. I didn't even know I was going to throw it until I threw it. It was pure luck. He said he was going to bury me in that graveyard. That woman said they killed another woman. And baby! I wanted to get out of there alive, with the baby."

"We're going to have to hold you," Bjerke said.

Cash stared at him.

"Can I get you to stand up and walk back to the cell we had you in earlier? The deputy here will escort you."

Cash, stunned, got up without a word and walked back to the cell. This time, the door was closed and locked with a metal key. Cash dropped her butt on the hard bed and glared at the deputy as he stood staring back at her. He was the first to look away. His footsteps echoed back down the hallway.

She hollered after him, "Let the dog outta my truck." *Well, what the hell.* "Hey, hey, you there. Tell him to call Sheriff Wheaton in Ada."

The footsteps continued away from the cell.

Cash sat on the bed for the rest of the day. She toyed with the idea of using the screwdriver to try to pick the lock. Instead she stuck it under the mattress, thinking, *I might need this for something else later.* She got up once or twice and asked to use the bathroom down the hall. At least they had the decency to let her do that. Even if it meant she could feel the deputy standing outside the bathroom door.

Deputy Bjerke brought her a turkey sandwich he said his wife made for her. He told her the baby was doing fine when Cash asked.

After Cash ate, and used the bathroom again, she sat on the hard bed and shut her thoughts to all that had happened. She focused her mind until all was still in the universe. At first, it was a fine fog that enveloped her. She floated out of her body. She looked down and saw herself on a metal bed in the brick jailhouse. She floated up and out and over the small town. The night air was crisp, and the stars shone brightly. Cash soared over the tamarack forest until she saw a plume of smoke rising through the treetops. She followed the smoke down and floated on the ceiling of Jonesy's house. Jonesy sat at the table eating a bowl of tomato soup and saltine crackers.

"Visiting around, are you?"

"Nothing better to do."

"You did the right thing, girl. It's going to be okay."

"*Really?*"

"*You have powerful spirits watching out for you.*"

"*Maybe they fell asleep. I'm sitting in a jail cell. They say I murdered him.*"

"*Wheaton's back. You should visit him.*"

And just like that, Cash's spirit zipped west across the tamaracks, down into the valley thirty miles as the crow flies across the unplowed fields. She found herself hovering in the treetops outside Wheaton's house. He was bent over Gunner. He petted and stroked the dog. "Hey, where you been? How'd you get so muddy? Are you out there chasing skunks? Raccoons? I get home and they say they haven't seen you in a day or two." Gunner looked up and barked at Cash.

Wheaton rubbed the dog's neck. "Shh, you'll wake the neighbors. You had me worried. Get in the house. You look worse than when I found you in that gunny sack running down the road. You need to get some food and water in you. Good dog." Gunner looked up at Cash and barked one more time before going into the house.

Sometime during the night Cash must have lain down and covered herself with the scratchy wool blanket from the end of the bed because she woke up prone and covered when the early morning sun entered the cell. Her head was on a pillow with barely any fluff left to it. She couldn't hear any human movement from any part of the jail. She wasn't ready to interact with anyone, either. So, as much as it disgusted her, Cash pushed off the bed and walked to the toilet bolted to the concrete wall. She dropped her pants halfway to her knees and forced the pee out as fast as she could, then quickly stood and zipped her jeans back up. Thankful that no one had passed by and that the rest of the cells were empty. Not wanting to call attention to herself, she didn't bother to flush the toilet.

She retreated back to the bed, where she pulled the itchy blanket up to her shoulders and ran the events of the past few days over and over in her head. She reached under the mattress and got her screwdriver. Stuck it back up her jacket sleeve. Just in case. Then she used her mind to send messages to Wheaton to come get her. She was pretty sure he didn't know how to hear her, but she tried anyway.

Her internal clock told her it was about seven in the morning when the jail secretary walked back with a deputy. She carried a tray of food with a cup of coffee. Cash got up and walked to the cell door. The deputy unlocked it and the woman handed Cash the tray. At the sight of oatmeal and buttered toast, Cash's stomach growled. She took the tray to the bed and sat down. The woman retreated and the deputy locked the cell. Cash jumped off the bed and reached the door before the deputy could turn away.

"Call Sheriff Wheaton over in Ada."

"Why?"

"He'll vouch for me. Please. Call him. Tell someone to call him."

The deputy walked away without answering.

Cash yelled after him, "Hey, don't I get one phone call? I'm supposed to get one phone call." She thumped back on the flat mattress. She ate the breakfast and drank the coffee before it got cold. Finished, she placed the tray on the floor by the door and went back to the bed, where she pushed her back up against the wall and started breathing deep to go back into a meditative state. *No point in staying awake in this shithole.*

Jangling keys and metal scraping on metal jerked her back into her physical body.

"Come on. Bjerke wants to talk to you."

Cash rushed out of the cell and followed the deputy down the hall. She was taken into the same room she had been questioned in the day before. This time, it was just Bjerke and one tribal cop.

They all sat quietly for a few uncomfortable minutes. Cash was damned if she was going to talk first. She slouched in the chair. First, she picked at the loose threads in the hole of her jacket. Then she chewed the fingernails off her left hand. She pulled off a hangnail on the ring finger and a tiny drop of blood appeared. The tribal cop paced the room. Between strides, he would stand at the one window and look out. Cash's stomach growled. It had to be close to noon. She could hear the occasional crackle of a walkie-talkie and the low murmur as someone talked on a phone. Anytime anyone walked on the marble floor of the hallway, their footsteps echoed.

Bjerke stopped scribbling on the pad of paper in front of him. He motioned to the tribal cop that he could leave. Bjerke looked at Cash. She stared back, sat up straight.

"We talked to the folks in Ada. Sheriff Wheaton is on his way over here."

Cash's heart leaped. She did not want to go back into the cell.

He fiddled with his pencil and tapped the table with the eraser. "What name did the pastor's wife give you?"

"Lillian, Lily, then Lil. She kept changing names."

"She told us her name was Lillian Steene. Her husband is . . . was Pastor John Steene."

"Yeah."

"She says she doesn't remember anything from the other night. She doesn't remember you or a baby."

"That's not possible." Cash leaned forward at the table.

Bjerke shrugged. "We went through the house. We found some baby clothes, diapers and stuff in the upstairs bedroom. We found the pushed-out screen of the basement window."

Cash nodded slowly.

"Why did they have the baby?" he asked.

"I don't know." She leaned forward in the chair. "I think they're crazy. Like really crazy, not just normal crazy. He said the baby was his. She said 'Lillian' killed the baby's mom. That the baby was born in DL. And that 'Lil' killed two other babies."

Bjerke shook his head, then looked at Cash with skepticism. "Whose baby is it, really?"

"She's not mine, for God's sake," Cash said, her eyes growing big. "They stole her. From a woman named Edie. The baby's mom is Edie Birch. Except, she is dead too. They killed her. I brought the baby here, where she'd be safe. You have to find the rest of her family."

"Wheaton said he looks out for you. And that you helped them solve a murder a bit ago."

Cash nodded.

"He said you brought those girls back from the cities that were being pimped down there."

Cash nodded again.

"You killed a man."

Cash didn't react.

"Last night you killed a man."

Cash just stared at him.

"And we don't know for sure whose baby this is."

Cash still didn't move.

"Wheaton is on his way over here to take you back to Ada. He'll keep an eye on you until he brings you back to get arraigned on the murder charge."

Cash didn't move. "Murder? I didn't try to kill him."

"You'll get a chance to say that to a judge. Tell me again about his wife and the baby?"

Cash looked out the window and thought through the past week. After a long silence, Deputy Bjerke coughed to get her attention. She turned to him. "Lily said that Lillian killed her. But Lillian is Lil. And Lily is both of them. I tell you, that woman is crazy. But Edie was the baby's mom. Her family just buried her up by Lake George."

Bjerke clicked some buttons on the walkie-talkie that was sitting on the table. "Can you send the tribal cop back in here?" More crackling from the walkie-talkie. Footsteps echoed in the hall, coming closer.

"Tell him what you just told me."

Cash did. The tribal cop didn't say anything. He just turned and left.

Bjerke stood up from the table. "As soon as Wheaton's here, you can leave. We'll talk with him upfront first. Fill him in. I'll send the secretary in with a sandwich and some more coffee."

Cash nodded.

He left the room. The secretary came in shortly after and put a plate with an egg salad sandwich in front of Cash. She asked Cash if she wanted some coffee. Cash nodded and lit up a cigarette before she devoured the sandwich.

It seemed like forever, but maybe it was only an hour before Wheaton showed up. Cash sensed his arrival before she heard his voice as he conversed with Bjerke down the hall. She wiped bread crumbs off the table and smoked another cigarette while she waited.

Wheaton entered the room, hand on the loop where his handcuffs hung. For a moment, Cash thought he was going to put the handcuffs on her. Instead, he tilted his head toward the door as a signal for her to follow him out. Outside, she took a deep breath of the cool spring air. A robin hopped on the courthouse lawn. A pickup passed on the street with hay bales stacked in the back end of it. Gunner's head was visible through the windshield of Wheaton's car.

The last time Cash had seen Gunner, he was sitting in the passenger seat of her Ranchero. "What's Gunner doing in your car?"

Wheaton didn't answer. He went to the passenger side and let the dog out. Gunner ran around the courthouse lawn until he found a place to do his business. When the dog finished and ran back to the car, Wheaton said, "He wasn't at the house when I got home. The neighbor, who was supposed to watch him, said Gunner disappeared the other day. She said she didn't know what happened to him. Said he showed up late last night, grubby, mud up to his belly. And starving. You wouldn't know anything about this, would you?" Gunner stood by Wheaton before he took one brief look at Cash and jumped in Wheaton's car. Cash didn't answer, just stared at the dog that now ignored her.

"Follow me," Wheaton said as he got into the brown and tan county sedan. She couldn't tell if he was angry with her or not. He had never been mad at her before. But he was so quiet now that she was worried.

Cash got into the Ranchero. She retrieved the screwdriver from her jacket sleeve and pushed it under the seat before she fiddled with the cut wires until the engine kicked on. She lifted a hand to signal to Wheaton she was ready to go. She chain-smoked all the way to Ada. Didn't turn the radio on. She just smoked and drove. She followed Wheaton into the parking lot of the Norman county jail. Cash sat in the truck, window rolled down, and waited for him to approach.

"You okay?"

Cash nodded. That seemed to be all she was doing today.

"Anything you want to talk about right now?"

She shook her head no.

"We're going to have to go back over there once they set a date and time with the court. They let you out on your own personal recognizance, based on my word."

She nodded yes.

"You sure you're okay?"

She nodded again.

He slapped her car door. "Stay outta trouble between now and then."

Cash nodded once more. Gunner stuck his head out of Wheaton's car window, looked at her, then turned away. She put the truck in first and eased out of the parking lot and south to Fargo after stopping at the local bar and getting another pack of cigarettes out of the machine that sat in the entryway.

She chain-smoked as she drove. It seemed like a lifetime ago since she had sat in a boat with Al, riding through the floodwaters that covered the valley. A lifetime since Wheaton had told her a woman had floated in with the flood and asked her to try to find out who the woman in the basement of the hospital might be. The drive to Devils Lake and back. She had forgotten to fill Wheaton in on finding out the woman was Lori White Eagle and that her family had probably already gotten her from the hospital. Cash couldn't bear the thought of turning around to go back to Ada and have another conversation with Wheaton.

When was the last time she had a beer? Shot a game of pool? Cash lit another cigarette off the butt she was smoking before she tossed it out the window. Then, out of habit, she reached over and felt under the car seat. A screwdriver, but still no bottle down there.

On the outskirts of Moorhead, she saw Al's house and garage up ahead. His pickup sat in the driveway. Without thought, she pulled in behind it. She finished her cigarette, then got out of her truck. Al came out of his garage, his hands wrapped in a dirty grease rag, a grin on his face that evaporated when he saw her.

"Hey."

"Hey."

"You okay? Looks like you've been in a fight or two."

She had forgotten what she must look like. Cash leaned over and looked at her reflection in the side-view mirror. The left side of her face had a slight bruise. She touched her cheek. She didn't even remember getting hit. Cash looked back at Al and shrugged.

"Come on in. Let me get you—"

"A beer. A beer."

"Sure enough."

She followed him into his house. He got a beer out of the fridge and handed it to her. She gulped half of it, standing.

"Hey, come on. Sit down."

"Nah." She took another big gulp, then walked through the living room to his bathroom. As soon as she shut the door, she leaned over the toilet and threw up until she was retching with dry heaves.

Al pushed the door open enough to poke his head in. "Hey, you all right?"

Cash dropped to the floor and retched again.

"Sorry, but you look like a train hit you. Why don't you hop in the shower?" He disappeared for a couple minutes, then pushed a clean towel through the door. After he closed it, Cash sat on the floor, spitting out more bile.

Finally, she stood, stripped, stepped into the tub and allowed hot water to pour down on her. She spent a long time with her head against the wall, saw in her mind's eye the knife being pulled from the pastor's neck and the spurt of blood that followed. She fought the gag that constricted her throat. When the water started to get cold, she stood under it as long as she could stand to. Then she stepped out of the shower. Sitting on the toilet lid was a T-shirt and some gray sweatpants. She dried off and put them on. They were way too big. She dug through the clothes on the floor and found her jean jacket and pulled that on.

Al was standing right outside the bathroom door when she opened it.

"Better?"

She shook her head no. He pulled her into his arms. Cash started to shiver. Then shake. Her whole body shook. Her teeth chattered. She couldn't talk.

Al picked her up and took her into the bedroom. He laid her on the bed and wrapped a quilt around her. Then he lay down and held her while she shook. At some point, she gasped. Took big gulps of air.

"What happened?"

"I killed a guy." She gulped more air.

Al kept holding her.

Cash was disoriented when she woke up. It took her a moment to remember where she was and why. She sat up in the bed and pulled the quilt tightly around her, even though the shaking had stopped. The room was dark, except for the light of a small lamp that had been left on. The clock on the nightstand read 8:12. She shook her head and rubbed her eyes. She didn't hear Al moving in other parts of the house. Gingerly, she got off the bed, quilt still wrapped around her. She pulled the curtain and shade back off the window and peeked out. It was light out. She looked back at the clock: 8:14. *What day is it?*

Al wasn't in the living room—the TV was on, but the sound was off. Cash walked through the empty kitchen, then headed outside. It was morning. *I slept all day and night?* Al came out of the garage, same old dirty grease rag in his hands. "There you are. Come on back into the house. I'll fry you up an egg."

He sat quietly at the table with her while she ate an over-easy egg and a piece of toast. After she took the last bite and washed it down with a cup of coffee, she proceeded to tell him everything that happened at the church on the prairie. She didn't tell him about the dark shadow or the time when it felt like she was in the fourth dimension. Her mind hadn't made sense of that for her own self, but she did tell him about the pastor and his wife and the baby. He didn't say anything. He got up once and refilled their coffee cups. Another time, he went into the bedroom and Cash could hear him opening and closing drawers. When he returned, he had a new pack of Pall Mall straights. He took two out, lit them both, handed her one and smoked the other himself.

When she was done with the story, they sat in silence. They drank black coffee and smoked cigarettes. Finally, Al broke the silence. "I fixed your truck. Got those wires back up under the dash. I put your keys on your clothes in the bedroom. I'm gonna go back out and finish this carburetor I need to rebuild. No need to hurry or go anyplace." He left the kitchen.

Cash put her head on her arms on the table. Once again, images of the knife flying through the air, the blood spurting, herself grabbing the baby and running replayed in her mind. Lillian's, or whoever the hell she was, skirt flying up over her bare legs as she chased Cash down the gravel road. *Damn!*

Cash sat up and went into the bedroom. She got dressed, grabbed her keys and went out to the truck. She opened the driver's door and saw that it looked as if nothing had ever happened to it. She stuck the keys in the ignition before she went into the garage. Al had a carburetor up on a workbench. Screwdriver in his hand. Cash felt a giggle rise in her throat but shoved it down. "What?"

"Nothin'. I gotta get home."

As if reading her mind, Al said, "I wouldn't go to the Casbah if I were you. Why don't you grab what's left of the six-pack in my fridge and just go home and crawl into bed again?"

Cash didn't argue. She grabbed the beer and headed across the river to her apartment, where once inside, she opened a beer and ate a piece of toast after cutting off the mold from one side of the crust. She played game after game of solitaire. As she slapped down cards, she willed her mind to go blank. When she lost the game to the devil, she locked the screen door and the inside door. Even though it was still daylight out, she turned on all the lights in the apartment, even the one in the bathroom, and left the door open. The last thing she wanted to do was wake up in the dark. She willed herself not to think as she got undressed down to her panties and T-shirt. She crawled into bed with the last bottle of beer and five cigarettes left in the pack.

When Cash woke again, the clock on her dresser read 6:23. It took her a bit to realize she had slept most of a day and a whole night. Coffee. Cigarette. Pee. Hairbrush. Get dressed. For the first time ever, she dialed Wheaton's number on her phone.

"Hello?"

"It's me."

"How you doing?"

"Okay."

Silence.

"What day is it?"

"Wednesday."

"I have to go to school."

"Go to school, Cash."

"Okay. Am I going to go to prison?" The telephone cord was wrapped so tightly around her wrist that it was cutting the circulation off her fingers. She unwound the cord.

"No, Cash, you are not going to prison. Go to school."

Cash hung up. She put on the rest of her clothes, filled her Thermos and went to school. She had missed the first two days of classes after spring break and had to run around and find the right rooms, find the right teachers, get the right syllabus. She went to the registrar's office and dropped judo from her class schedule. *Fuck judo*, she thought as she signed the necessary paperwork.

Mrs. Kills Horses chased her down in a hallway and reminded her that, in order to keep her BIA scholarship monies, she needed to be registered for a full course load. She *tsk-tsk*'d over Cash's black and blue cheekbone. Cash said she ran into her bathroom door in the dark. Mrs. Kills Horses all but rolled her eyes. Cash said her goodbyes and went back to the registrar's office to sign up for Criminal Justice 101.

She found Sharon eating french fries in the Student Union. "Come on, shoot a game of pool."

Sharon rolled her eyes too. "What truck did you run into?" When Cash ignored her, she said, "Sure, let's shoot pool; I'll be your guppy, and you'll be my shark." Cash didn't know where Sharon got all her flippant sayings, probably from the hippie bunch she hung out with. Cash led the way to a pool table in the rec hall and racked. Sharon broke and balls scattered. A stripe and a solid dropped.

"Your choice," Cash said.

Sharon leaned across the table; her miniskirt riding dangerously high. She took aim at another solid that was sitting right on the rim of a corner pocket. The cue ball followed the solid as it dropped. "Damn!"

"Tables still open. I'll take stripes since you already made two solids. Give you a chance."

Sharon talked nonstop about some pot she and her boyfriend had smoked over break. "Best pot ever." Cash just listened and shot pool.

"Here comes some competition," Sharon said just as Cash dropped the 8-ball in the side pocket. She looked up and saw Bunk and Tezhi approach.

"You didn't even say goodbye," said Bunk. "We woke up, and you were gone."

Cash shrugged and pointed at the cue sticks on the wall. "Let's play partners. Me and Sharon against the two of you."

"Who beat you up?" asked Tezhi.

Cash touched her cheek.

"You didn't snag that Nodin brother after I told you not to?" exclaimed Bunk.

"No."

"So, what happened?"

"I tripped into my bathroom door."

"That's what they all say. Stay away from the Nodin boys."

Cash shook her head and broke up the triangle of balls that sat at the other end of the table. Nothing dropped. "Your turn," she said.

The four played until the Union shut down for the evening. Cash welcomed their constant chatter. They laughed and made up tall tales of how Cash got into a fight and what the other person must look like. Cash didn't bother to tell the truth. When Bunk said she saw Cash's name with Shyla's on the sign-up board for the women's pool tournament, she said she would have to check it out.

Cash went to the Casbah and sipped two beers the remainder of the night. She brushed off Jim when he asked to come over at closing time. She went home alone and slept with all the lights on again.

Cash got into a rhythm of classes, an occasional field to plow as the fields dried up, and nightly pool games back at the Casbah. The lights in her apartment stayed on constantly, to the point where she had to make a run to the hardware store for some new bulbs. At school, Mrs. Kills Horses pestered her about her grades. Ever since Cash won a state writing contest, Mrs. Kills Horses didn't miss a chance to let someone, anyone, know about her star "Indian" student. And she was adamant that Cash continue to perform at her "fullest potential."

Once a week, Cash stopped at the jail in Ada and checked in with Wheaton. Each time she went to the jail, Gunner would look up at her and then look away. Cash always patted his head and said under her breath, "Go ahead, pretend you don't know me." She finally told Wheaton about Lori White

Eagle. He had already gotten a call from Dick over at Devils Lake and knew the story.

One afternoon, Wheaton told her to get in his car and they drove over to Twin Valley. They sat in a booth, and he ordered roast beef sandwiches and apple pie for both of them. Cash still wondered and looked for a hint at whether what Geno said was true or not, that Wheaton had a girlfriend in Twin Valley. Cash tried to watch the waitress when she came to their table to see if any signals passed between them. She couldn't tell. And with Geno still in the southwest at art school, she couldn't ask him.

Wheaton asked her to tell him again what happened at the church. Cash did. She left out the part where she forgot she had a screwdriver up her sleeve that she could have used as a weapon. Just thinking about it made her chest tighten with a squashed-down giggle. Same with the roadrunner woman. She sometimes had nightmares of Lillian as she ran down the road, skirt flying up around her waist as she chased Cash and Gunner. She also didn't tell Wheaton how she had picked Gunner up to ride shotgun for her. Gunner couldn't talk; why should she?

"The pastor's wife kept changing her name?"

"You should have seen her face." She talked around a mouthful of apple pie. "She has a different face. And a different voice that appears with each name."

"Darnedest thing I've ever heard."

They both sipped coffee, deep in thought.

Wheaton broke the silence. "And they took that woman's

baby? I heard about these nuns up in Canada who would put newborn babies in men's shoeboxes. Those big boxes our work boots come in? They shipped Indian babies across the border and sold them to white people to adopt down here in the States. When the mothers asked for their babies, the nuns said they died at birth."

Cash stared at Wheaton.

"Sometimes the world just makes no darn sense, Cash."

"How can they say they're Christians?"

Wheaton just shook his head. "There are other horror stories of priests getting girls pregnant at the Indian boarding schools and then the nuns killing the babies. There is evil in the world, Cash. You know that. Has nothing to do with the devil. Or God. Human beings do some pretty awful things sometimes, and sometimes they use God as their excuse, or the devil, rather than taking responsibility for their own actions."

Cash shook her head in disbelief. Took another sip of coffee.

"Want to tell me again about Devils Lake and Lori White Eagle?" Wheaton asked.

Cash did. She left out the part about Doc Felix cornering her in the refrigerated room. She left out the part about the Shell Lake party and the tire fire too.

"How's school?"

"I'm taking criminal justice."

"That's good. That's real good."

When they were done talking, long after they finished

eating, Cash stepped outside and stood in the entryway to wait while Wheaton paid for the meal. She stepped around to the front window so she could see him and the waitress at the cash register. Cash thought the way the waitress tilted her head might mean she was flirting with him.

When Wheaton turned to leave, Cash quickly stepped back up on the entryway step. She didn't want him to find her spying on him. Neither talked on the way back to Ada. Everything that had needed to be talked about was said while they ate and drank their coffee. They watched the fields and farmhouses roll by in quietude.

"Stay in touch," he said as he stood by the door of her Ranchero once they arrived in Ada.

"I will."

Cash drove toward the edge of town and changed her mind. She figured she had another good hour before sunset. Enough time to find Jonesy's house in the woods. It wasn't until she was on the gravel road in the forest that she turned her headlights on. She put out her cigarette and rolled down the driver's side window. The air smelled of springtime dampness, pine trees and forest floor. And there it was, the smell of woodstove smoke. Cash slowed and began to watch the side of the road for the turn into Jonesy's driveway. Her headlights created a bright path in the darkness. A steady stream of bugs was caught in the beam of light. Once, a pair of deer eyes looked out from the trees that hugged the road.

Cash turned into the driveway that approached on the left. Ahead, a small window cast light out into the parking space beside the small shack. The click of the Ranchero door as it shut was an intrusive foreign sound of metal on metal when all the other sounds were quiet nature sounds. Before Cash could knock on the door, Jonesy opened it and stepped back for her to enter. She motioned for Cash to go ahead and sit at the table. Cash sat while Jonesy fussed around with water and a metal pot on the stove. Eventually, she brought two cups of tea to the table and sat across from Cash.

"Had some adventures, have you?"

Cash told her the story of being at the pastor's that night with Lillian and the baby and the dark shadow. She didn't even leave out the part about seeing Jonesy float into the room and tell Cash not to show fear. Jonesy nodded to let Cash know what she had experienced was real. Then she got up and refilled their teacups.

"How did you know where to find me?" Cash asked Jonesy.

"You know, my girl, some things we can't answer. We just know. And we have to take care of the knowing. And we have to take care of each other. Not everything can be explained the way the schools or the churches would want us to think they can be."

The warm liquid felt comforting as Cash drank it down. She nodded at Jonesy to let her know she heard her. Then she grinned. "Speaking of school, I have class tomorrow. I quit judo. No one sticks their arms out and says, 'Here, twist it behind my back.'" They both laughed.

Cash also told her about the Phillips screwdriver, how

she had forgotten she had it and ended up with a useless, dull butter knife before finding a paring knife in a drawer. By this time, she was taking deep breaths, trying hard not to burst with laughter. "That stupid paring knife. I was like one of those knife throwers at the county fair. Whoow! Right through the air and into his neck."

Tears rolled down Cash's cheeks. She couldn't stop. Every time she opened her eyes and looked at Jonesy, she got the giggles all over.

When Cash stopped to gasp for air, Jonesy said, "You did what?"

"I forgot I put the screwdriver up my sleeve to use as a weapon. Totally. Forgot. I. Had. It." And she was off again, shoulders shaking, tears threatening to fall from her eyes. "And you should have seen that woman running after me. Skirt flying up. She looked like the roadrunner from cartoons." Cash doubled over, crossed her arms across her stomach and laughed uncontrollably. "I'm gonna pee my pants," she said between breaths, brushing the tears off her cheeks. "A fucking roadrunner."

Jonesy got up and came back with a glass of water. "Take a drink. A roadrunner, aye?"

Cash took a quick sip, then put her head on her arms on the table, back to uncontrollable giggles, which quickly turned to sobs. After many long minutes, she finally caught her breath.

Back in control of her emotions, Cash lifted her head from her arms. She wiped the tears off her cheeks and blew her nose on a big red hanky Jonesy handed her. "Really, I'm all right." She drained the water from the glass.

"I know."

"I didn't mean to kill him."

"I know."

"I don't want to go to prison."

"You won't."

"You sure?"

"I'm sure."

"I didn't mean to kill him."

"It's going to be okay, my girl. Really, it is."

"I gotta get home. I have class in the morning."

"Take it easy. Don't worry too much about all this." Jonesy picked up the cups and glasses and put them in the sink. "You did the right thing. The baby will stay with her grandma over here on the reservation. I think that lady will end up at the state hospital over in Fergus Falls, if she isn't already there. And that pastor? He is where he belongs—in the ground. You go home and rest. Do your schoolwork. Win that pool tournament and bring me the trophy."

It was the most words Cash had heard Jonesy speak at one time.

Jonesy handed her a flashlight and tilted her head toward the door. Cash went out and used the outhouse. She brought the flashlight back to Jonesy and got in the Ranchero to drive back to Fargo. Jonesy stood in her doorway, light spilling out from behind her. Cash felt Jonesy watching her drive away.

Back in Fargo, Cash stopped at the Casbah. Shorty slid her

a Bud across the oak bar counter. She sipped it while going to the pool table to put her quarters up. She passed Ol' Man Willie, who sat slouched in his booth, a half-empty glass of beer on the table in front of him as he nodded off. Jim lifted his cue stick in greeting as Cash got to the table, a signal that they should shoot as partners. She nodded yes. It was an easy night of slow drinks, the clatter of dropped billiard balls and the occasional two-step on the wood floor in front of the jukebox.

When Cash left at closing time, Jim followed her out. She stopped when she reached her Ranchero and turned to look at him. His blond hair in a farmer cut—close-shaved around the neck, parted on the side and combed over. He was wearing a flannel lined jean jacket over a plaid cotton shirt. Blue jeans were snug on his hips. His blue eyes sparkled in the neon light from the bar. He looked at Cash with confidence. "I'll follow you."

Cash looked again at his blond hair and blue eyes. His eagerness to get to her bed overrode the fact that he would then go home to his wife. She looked at him, assessed his thin stature that didn't promise to protect her. He had never asked what she did outside of drink, drive truck, shoot pool, and have sex with him. And she had never felt any wish to share anything with him other than her body, and then only every once in a while. "No, not now," she said and got into the Ranchero. She pulled the door shut behind her and left him standing on the pavement.

The rest of the week was classes, a plowed field for one

of the farmers outside of Hendrum and nights at the Casbah till closing time. On Thursday, she was in the Student Union shooting pool against herself when Shyla and Terry walked in.

"Hey."

"Bunk said we would find you here. Wanna play 9-ball?" Terry asked.

"Sure. Rack 'em up."

"You ready for the tournament this weekend?" Shyla asked.

"This weekend?"

"Yeah. We hadn't seen you around. But here," she said, pulling a black shirt out of the paper bag she carried. The shirt had turquoise and red ribbons sewn across the back, along with two-foot-long streams of ribbon that hung down. "I made us matching shirts."

Cash didn't know what to do. She reached out for the shirt but then dropped her hand. She looked around the Union as if to make sure there was an exit.

"Here. I hope it fits. I know you're much smaller than me. I kinda had to guess at your size." She put the shirt in Cash's hand.

Cash didn't dare look at Shyla. Her chest felt full, and her eyes stung. She didn't remember ever getting a gift from anyone other than Wheaton, and that was usually a very practical itchy wool sweater at Christmastime. Without looking up, she held the shirt to her shoulders. "It'll fit," she said.

"Mine is just like it. We haven't figured out how to get 'Al's Auto' on it yet." Shyla laughed.

"Let's play 9-ball," Terry interjected.

They played until the Union closed for the night. Terry and Shyla headed back to Concordia after they walked with Cash to her Ranchero. She offered to give them a ride to campus, but they said they'd rather walk. "See you Saturday for the tournament. Starts at one—don't be late," Shyla hollered back as they headed across the campus lawn. Cash was up early on Saturday morning. She tried on the ribbon shirt—soft black fabric. She leaned over the kitchen table, pretending she had a cue stick in her hand. The ribbons floated down to the side. They didn't catch in the swing of her arm at all. She took the shirt off and put on a T-shirt, then headed over to the Silver Spoon and had breakfast and a cup of coffee. She read the *Fargo Forum*, back to front, as was her usual habit.

Back at her apartment, she straightened up the clean clothes on the chair and the dirty clothes on the floor. She swept all the floors and pushed the dirt out the door. She washed the few plates and cups in the kitchen sink. She even rinsed out the coffee pot and Thermos. She didn't know why she felt so nervous. Shooting pool was the one thing she knew how to do. Some of the men in the bars joked that she could shoot pool blindfolded and still win.

But this was different. Shyla was counting on her. To make matters worse, there would be no beer being served at the billiard hall. Cash went to her fridge and pulled out a Bud, but when she went to open the bottle, she stopped. She just looked at it. Shyla and Terry didn't drink. No one would drink all afternoon. Cash put the beer back in the fridge.

With nothing left to do with all her nervous energy, she got dressed and drove to the billiard hall.

It was 12:30 when she arrived. Shyla looked beautiful in her ribbon shirt that matched Cash's; she even had a single braid down her back like Cash. Shyla waved her over. "I was getting nervous. Thought you might have gotten cold feet. The shirt fits good."

"Thank you. Do we get some practice games?"

"Yep, I'll re rack," Shyla said. She scooped the balls on the table into the rack. "You break. Terry will be over after he finishes his work-study job at the campus gym. Where's Al?"

Cash shrugged and broke the balls. Three stripes dropped. "Hope that's my luck for the day," she said as she aimed at another stripe. She ran the table.

"Whoo-hoo!" said Shyla as she racked the balls. "We got this!"

And they did. Terry arrived during their first match. Al arrived shortly after. The guys kept a steady supply of pitchers of Coke for themselves and Shyla and a pitcher of ice water for Cash on the side table. They cheered the women on and shit-talked at the other teams the women played. Shyla and Cash never lost a game all afternoon.

It wasn't that the other teams were all that bad, but the reality was, Shyla and Cash were just *that good*. Their winnings were $125 each and an offer to go to the State Tournament, backed by Clyde's Billiards. They each got a trophy to commemorate their win. Afterward, they went out to eat at Shari's Kitchen, where they, once again, laughed as they replayed each game, each missed shot, and each winning 8-ball shot while eating French dip sandwiches.

Al convinced Cash to go with him to a bar in Moorhead close to his place after Terry and Shyla headed back to their dorms. First, Cash went back to her apartment and changed out of the ribbon shirt. *My good luck shirt*, she thought as she smoothed it over the back of the chair in her bedroom.

She met Al at his suggested bar. He was seated in a booth with two bottles of beer on the table. "The pool table's lined up with quarters. We're tenth in line."

He talked about a truck engine he was working on. She talked about what fields she needed to plow for the next week or so. She told him she quit her judo class. "Fuck judo and butter knives." They both laughed. When their quarters were up, they played and won until closing time. She went with him to his house.

At three in the morning, she rolled to the edge of his bed, sheet wrapped up around her armpits. She lit a cigarette and sipped the bottled beer that sat on the nightstand.

"Gotta go," was all she said.

Al lit a cigarette and watched her get dressed. As she left the bedroom, he said, "See you later, Cash. Congratulations on your win." She grinned back at him and gave a short wave.

Back across the river in her upstairs apartment, she ran the ribbons of the shirt through her hands and smoothed the shirt down. *My good luck shirt*, and crawled into bed. She still slept with all the lights on.

On Sunday morning, she did laundry and homework. In the afternoon, she drove up to Hendrum and talked to a couple farmers who had put the word out they needed farm help in the coming week. One had a job cleaning out his haymow. She told him she would come out on Thursday and get the job done. She ran over to Jonesy's and delivered her trophy. Told her she didn't have time to have a cup of tea—she needed to get back to Fargo because she had class in the morning.

Back in her apartment, she grabbed a beer and a fresh pack of cigarettes, got undressed down to her panties and T-shirt. She crawled into bed with her criminal justice textbook. This week's assignment was about the history of search seizures as outlined in the US Constitution. She was deep into the subject when her phone rang.

Two rings. Silence. Three rings. Silence. *Wheaton.* Cash jumped out of bed when the phone rang again, two rings. Silence. Before the third ring, Cash answered, "Hello."

"Cash, Wheaton here."

"Yeah."

"They called me from Mahnomen. Lillian Steene has a hearing this week for kidnapping the baby."

"Oh." She wound the phone cord around her arm from the elbow to her wrist.

"We've been asked to be over there. They want you there on Thursday."

"Why me? Are they going to throw me back in jail?"

"I don't think so, Cash. Sounds like the hearing is to

determine whether to prosecute her or not. Depends on what she has to say. You may not have to go to court at all."

Cash was silent. She wrapped the phone cord tighter around her arm.

"Cash, I don't think you have anything to worry about. Come to Ada tomorrow after school. The county attorney is going to be here to ask you a few questions. Walk you through questions you might be asked. Relative to the case."

"Wheaton!"

"He's on our side, Cash. On *your* side. I'm telling you, just be honest. Tell the truth. You have nothing to worry about. Tomorrow. When is your last class?"

"I get done around two-thirty."

"Okay. We'll see you a little after three then."

Cash hung up the phone. She barely slept. She would doze off, wake up and read some more criminal law. Look in the index for murder cases. For kidnapping cases. She would fall back asleep and wake up, her hand holding her place in the book.

In the morning, she crawled out of bed, filled her clean Thermos with coffee, gathered her stack of books and notebooks, then went to school.

In foster homes, there were days and nights that were hell on earth—times she would fall asleep hoping to not wake up, or almost convincing herself life was a dream and dreamtime was the real time. Her one respite during all those years was compulsory education. That was a rule even the foster families didn't dare break.

For Cash, school was a place where she could find some peace. Use her mind. Show off her smarts. So, that is what Cash did on Monday. She went to school and used her mind, shutting off any thought about Wheaton or court or a county attorney or Lillian and kidnapped babies. And definitely not about murder.

She did her studies. She walked through the brick hallways that still closed in on her. The stuffy rooms made her long for the open fields of the prairie and fresh air, the smell of muddy water and river vegetation floating up and away from the banks of the Red River. She heard Mrs. Kills Horses talking loudly in a classroom and quickly turned down another hall to avoid an encounter with her. She went early to her criminal justice class and sat in the empty room. She reread the chapters due and occasionally looked out the window at the oak trees that almost touched the glass. She saw a sparrow hop along a branch, noticed a student walking across campus, a guitar slung over his shoulder.

After class she drove to Ada and endured questions thrown at her by the county attorney. Wheaton sat with her. Cash had a giant headache by the time the ordeal was done. Wheaton offered to take her to Twin Valley to eat, but even the curiosity about him and a possible girlfriend didn't tempt Cash. She just wanted to get back to the safety of her apartment, and that is what she did.

THE NEXT FEW DAYS FOLLOWED in a blur. School in the morning. Each afternoon she drove to Ada for conversations with Wheaton about the hearing over in Mahnomen. He gave her money and told her to go to JCPenney and buy a dress and regular shoes to wear to the hearing. Cash didn't know why, if it was Lillian's hearing, she should be required to wear a dress.

When Cash showed up at the jail, wearing the JCPenney dress, to ride with Wheaton to the hearing on a Thursday, she was mortified. She felt naked and exposed. Wheaton did his best to assure her she looked just fine.

The hearing was in the courtroom in Mahnomen. Lillian was represented by a court-appointed attorney who wore an ill-fitting brown suit. An attendant from the Fergus Falls Asylum was present. Wheaton whispered to Cash that Lillian had been staying at the hospital in Fergus Falls until today.

A judge presided over the hearing. Cash sat at the back of the courtroom with Wheaton. The Mahnomen County Attorney questioned Lillian. As Lillian talked, Cash saw small flickers, twitches of her eyes, and the muscles around her mouth as she answered some questions. Then her face would twitch and Lil and/or Lily would answer. Each time, with each twitch that changed her face, Lillian's voice would also change.

Cash leaned forward, elbows on knees, chin in her hands. Fascinated. She looked at the judge. An old white man with white hair and gnarly knuckles that he cracked as he leaned back in his chair.

Lillian's court-appointed lawyer nervously shuffled papers on the table in front of him. He fidgeted, as if trying to stay in the same lane as his client. Lillian sat up straight and answered questions in full, clear sentences. Lil flipped her hair around and crossed her legs seductively. Lily had a sweet, soft voice. Cash poked Wheaton on his leg and asked with her eyes, *Are you seeing what I'm seeing?* He nodded yes, a puzzled look on his face.

Finally, the county attorney stopped and looked at the judge in puzzlement. Before he could utter a statement, Lily leaned forward. "Lil and John killed a baby before. And the babies' mothers. Well, Lillian killed the mothers. Lil put the babies to sleep. I guess, to be fair, John never killed anyone. He just buried them." She sat back, hands folded in her lap. She started to lean forward again, but this time, her lawyer jumped up and tried to stop her.

She looked at him with big, round eyes and said, "I want to go home. They said I would get to keep the baby. She"— she pointed at Cash in the back of the courtroom—"came to help me with the baby. Everything was fine . . ." Lillian got a lost look in her eyes, her voice got softer. Cash leaned forward again to hear her. "I don't know where John is. Where's my baby?" she asked the judge. Tears rolled down her face. The county attorney paced back to his table. Shuffled some papers. The judge cracked his knuckles.

Lillian's attorney asked to approach the bench. The judge beckoned him forward. They whispered, then the judge motioned for the county attorney to approach the bench. All three whispered to one another. Lily fidgeted on the witness stand. Cash watched Lillian appear for a fleeting second. Lil scanned the courtroom. She unbuttoned the top button of her shirtdress. Lily reached up and re-buttoned it.

Cash looked around the courtroom. There were maybe fifteen people altogether. At least one was a reporter from the paper in DL. Some were locals who had nothing better to do. None of the people looked familiar to Cash. No one from the church was present. No one seemed to notice the changes that flitted across the woman's face on the witness stand. Wheaton did. Both attorneys glanced at her several times in consternation. After a few more whispers, the judge told Lillian she could step down. As she did so, he hit his gavel on the bench, startling the woman, then said, "We're going to take a twenty-minute recess. Can I get the court reporter to join us back in the chambers?" And they all exited. Lillian was escorted by her attorney and the hospital attendant back into the judge's chambers.

"What's going on?" Cash asked Wheaton.

"I don't know. Darnedest thing I've ever seen."

Everyone left the courtroom and lit up a cigarette once they were out in the hallway. Cash and Wheaton stepped outside and down the courthouse steps to smoke theirs. Bjerke joined them. "Craziest thing I've ever seen," was all he said before lighting one for himself. They stood in silence, a soft spring breeze carrying the smoke away from them.

"They're coming back out," someone called from the courthouse doorway. Everyone stubbed out their cigarettes and filed back up the stairs and into the courtroom. The smell of cigarette smoke permeated the air inside. Cash slid in before Wheaton. The attorneys and Lillian were at their respective tables. The court reporter came in and sat at her typewriter. Someone said, "All rise," and the judge entered.

He sat down at the bench and looked out over the court-room. "This hearing will be continued to a later date after a more thorough evaluation of Mrs. Steene. Mrs. Steene will return to the Fergus Falls Asylum until it is deemed she is fully capable of understanding the proceedings against her and any possible charges that might be brought against her. You may all go home." He banged his gavel and exited the courtroom.

The room buzzed with speculation as two deputies crowded around Lillian and her attendant from the hospital. Lillian asked why and what was happening as they escorted the two of them out a side door.

Cash followed Wheaton out of the courthouse again. He stopped on the sidewalk to light up a cigarette. Cash followed suit. "What happened in there?" she asked.

"She's going back to Fergus for further evaluation." He shook his head. "Never seen anything like it."

Bjerke walked up just as they were getting ready to walk to their cars. "That woman's batshit crazy. I think it's pretty safe to say you don't have to worry about being charged with anything, Renee. You're supposed to go before the same judge next week."

Cash stared at Wheaton.

"I thought it best to get you through one ordeal at a time before you had to worry about a second one."

Cash stomped over to Wheaton's car and grabbed a paper

bag off the backseat. She walked back into the courthouse, stormed into the bathroom and changed back into jeans and a T-shirt. Then she stuffed the dress into the waste bin. She walked back out to Wheaton's car and sat sullenly in the passenger seat, waiting for him. She didn't talk to him all the way back to Ada, where she jumped into her Ranchero and drove away without so much as a wave goodbye.

The first thing she did when she got back to her apartment was yank the phone plug out of the wall. Then she threw the new shoes under the bed as hard as she could. She put on her tennis shoes, grabbed a beer from the fridge and drank it down. Cash got in her truck and drove to Hendrum. After she apologized to the farmer for being late to the job, she climbed in the haymow and worked until eleven-thirty at night, throwing hay bales around, rearranging them so they were easier to get at. When she was done, the farmhouse was dark. She got into her truck and a twenty-dollar bill was stuck in the ashtray.

Cash drove back to Fargo. It was too late to stop at the Casbah, so she went straight home, ran a bath and sat in the hot water long enough to drink a beer and smoke three cigarettes. She crawled into bed and fell sound asleep.

When she woke the next morning, she fell into a routine of classes, farm work when someone needed her, then pool and beer at the Casbah in the evenings. Al stopped by the Casbah one night and played a few games with her. Told her to plug her phone back in. She did. She and Shyla started playing pool each Saturday morning at the billiard hall to practice up for the State Tournament.

It was a cool spring night, just before dusk, when she saw Wheaton's car pull into the field turnoff. Cash rode a John Deere tractor that pulled a corn planter behind it. She was on the last corner of the last row in the field. She finished the turn and drove the tractor toward the car. He was sitting back on the hood, Gunner on the ground beside him.

"Still mad?" he asked.

"Nah, we're good."

"Bjerke called a couple weeks ago. Told me they aren't going to press charges against you. The pastor's wife is still in Fergus."

Cash nodded.

"He called again this morning. He said they arrested a guy this past weekend. Someone called Nodin. Drunk driving. His brothers bailed him out this morning. I told Bjerke about Lori White Eagle. Didn't give him the full story. Want to run over to Mahnomen with me tomorrow morning and tell him what we know?

"Well, dang. I guess, yeah."

Cash joined him as she leaned on the hood of his car. They both smoked a cigarette and watched the sun set.

AUTHOR'S NOTE

I have always been fascinated by the crimes that can happen in rural areas where people live isolated lives and tend to "stay out of other people's business." A number of years ago I was on a road trip. We had been driving forever without a town in sight when we saw a country church with a graveyard. We stopped for a break to stretch our legs and walked around the graveyard, which had two parts to it. One side was where Native Americans were buried—with names like Yellow Horse, Charging Buffalo and Standing Whirlwind. The other side was non-Native, with names like Johnson, Carlson or Smith. On that side I discovered a family plot where four children had all died before the parents, and all at a very young age. I called my friend over and said, "Look, someone murdered their children."

She said, "No! It must have been the flu pandemic." But

the dates were wrong and there was a pattern to how long the children lived and how far apart in age they were. My imagination went to an isolated mother suffering from post-partum depression or a rageful father. And out there, in the middle of nowhere, no one would be around to question an accident happening here, an illness occurring there.

Years later I sat down to write *Sinister Graves*. I finished the book before the world came to a pandemic standstill and before May 2021, when the remains of 215 children were found in unmarked graves at the Catholic-run Kamloops Boarding School grounds in British Colombia, Canada. The school had been in operation from 1890 to 1969, when the Canadian government took control. The number of children's bodies found at boarding schools across Canada since that time has risen to more than 1,100.

Canada's Truth and Reconciliation Commission, between 2007 and 2015, created a historical record of abuses within the boarding school system. "The TRC spent 6 years travelling to all parts of Canada and heard from more than 6,500 witnesses. The TRC also hosted 7 national events across Canada to engage the Canadian public, educate people about the history and legacy of the residential schools system, and share and honour the experiences of former students and their families." [https://www.rcaanccirnac.gc.ca/eng/1450124405 592/1529106060525]

Many of the survivors of the boarding school system who gave testimony at the TRC meetings spoke of children murdered at the schools. But an independent investigation was not done until 2021, when ground-penetrating radar was used and the unmarked graves were found.

Native Americans and First Nations people have always been expendable—from General Sheridan's "the only good Indian is a dead Indian" to Colonel Pratt's "kill the Indian, save the man" genocidal policies.

When I wrote *Sinister Graves*, I was well aware of the stories of abuses that the church perpetrated on our people during the boarding school era—and those of "good faith" who continued similar kinds of abuse within the foster care system prior to Congress's passing the Indian Child Welfare Act (ICWA) of 1978 to keep Indian children in Indian homes—but I was unprepared for the magnitude of children's bodies found on the numerous school grounds.

While this story isn't about a boarding school, it is about the twisted minds of people for whom Native children are expendable. And of course, Cash Blackbear does what she does to be of help. It is why this book is dedicated to #mmiw and #stolen children.

ACKNOWLEDGMENTS

Miigwech to so many people who have helped get me from there to here including my agent, Jacqui Lipton of Raven Quill Agency, along with the amazing team at Soho Press—Yezanira Venecia, Erica Loberg, Juliet Grames and Rachel Kowal, who all decided Cash Blackbear was worth the effort. As always, my friends Danny and Eileen, L'Jeanne's Grand Marais Writer's Residency, and my fellow writers of the Women From the Center writing group. My daughters, grandchildren and greats who are the driving force of my life, who are the multitude of reasons why I write and who give me the space and time to do so. Chi-miigwech to all who have gone before who hold me up and move me forward. And all you Native writers out there rock-starring it through the publishing world—thank you for being role models, inspiration and support on this journey.